Contemporary Fiction: A Very Short Introduction

VERY SHORT INTRODUCTIONS are for anyone wanting a stimulating and accessible way in to a new subject. They are written by experts, and have been published in more than 25 languages worldwide.

The series began in 1995, and now represents a wide variety of topics in history, philosophy, religion, science, and the humanities. The VSI library now contains more than 300 volumes—a Very Short Introduction to everything from ancient Egypt and Indian philosophy to conceptual art and cosmology—and will continue to grow in a variety of disciplines.

Very Short Introductions available now:

ADVERTISING Winston Fletcher
AFRICAN HISTORY
    John Parker and Richard Rathbone
AGNOSTICISM Robin Le Poidevin
AMERICAN HISTORY Paul S. Boyer
AMERICAN IMMIGRATION
    David A. Gerber
AMERICAN POLITICAL PARTIES
    AND ELECTIONS L. Sandy Maisel
AMERICAN POLITICS Richard M. Valelly
THE AMERICAN PRESIDENCY
    Charles O. Jones
ANAESTHESIA Aidan O'Donnell
ANARCHISM Colin Ward
ANCIENT EGYPT Ian Shaw
ANCIENT GREECE Paul Cartledge
ANCIENT PHILOSOPHY Julia Annas
ANCIENT WARFARE Harry Sidebottom
ANGELS David Albert Jones
ANGLICANISM Mark Chapman
THE ANGLO-SAXON AGE John Blair
THE ANIMAL KINGDOM
    Peter Holland
ANIMAL RIGHTS David DeGrazia
THE ANTARCTIC Klaus Dodds
ANTISEMITISM Steven Beller
ANXIETY Daniel Freeman and
    Jason Freeman
THE APOCRYPHAL GOSPELS
    Paul Foster
ARCHAEOLOGY Paul Bahn
ARCHITECTURE Andrew Ballantyne
ARISTOCRACY William Doyle
ARISTOTLE Jonathan Barnes

ART HISTORY Dana Arnold
ART THEORY Cynthia Freeland
ATHEISM Julian Baggini
AUGUSTINE Henry Chadwick
AUSTRALIA Kenneth Morgan
AUTISM Uta Frith
THE AVANT GARDE David Cottington
THE AZTECS David Carrasco
BARTHES Jonathan Culler
BEAUTY Roger Scruton
BESTSELLERS John Sutherland
THE BIBLE John Riches
BIBLICAL ARCHAEOLOGY
    Eric H. Cline
BIOGRAPHY Hermione Lee
THE BLUES Elijah Wald
THE BOOK OF MORMON
    Terryl Givens
BORDERS Alexander C. Diener and
    Joshua Hagen
THE BRAIN Michael O'Shea
BRITISH POLITICS Anthony Wright
BUDDHA Michael Carrithers
BUDDHISM Damien Keown
BUDDHIST ETHICS Damien Keown
CANCER Nicholas James
CAPITALISM James Fulcher
CATHOLICISM Gerald O'Collins
THE CELL Terence Allen and
    Graham Cowling
THE CELTS Barry Cunliffe
CHAOS Leonard Smith
CHILDREN'S LITERATURE
    Kimberley Reynolds

For more information visit our website
www.oup.com/vsi/

Robert Eaglestone

CONTEMPORARY FICTION

A Very Short Introduction

OXFORD
UNIVERSITY PRESS

OXFORD

UNIVERSITY PRESS

Great Clarendon Street, Oxford, OX2 6DP,
United Kingdom

Oxford University Press is a department of the University of Oxford.
It furthers the University's objective of excellence in research, scholarship,
and education by publishing worldwide. Oxford is a registered trade mark of
Oxford University Press in the UK and in certain other countries

British Library Cataloguing in Publication Data

Data available

ISBN 978-0-19-960926-0

Printed in Great Britain by
Ashford Colour Press Ltd, Gosport, Hampshire

To Poppy and to my friends

Contents

Acknowledgements

I want to thank many, many friends and colleagues for talking with me about fiction, especially: Eva Aldea, Matt Broadbent, Poppy Corbett, Jo Cottrell, Doug Cowie, Nemonie Craven, Elizabeth English, Malcolm Geere, Geraldine Glennon, Simon Glendinning, Sophie Goldsworthy, Judith Hawley, Nick Hoare, Henry Little, Kristen Krieder, Lynette Lukes, Ben Markovits, Martin MacQuillan, Judith Meddick, Kaye Mitchell, Adam Roberts, Dan Rebellato, Gavin Stewart, Danielle Sands, Hilary Sanders, Dan Stone, Richard Tennant, Carole Tonkinson, Emma Townshend, Nadia Valman.

I also want to thank Kerstin Demata, Emma Ma, Luciana O'Flaherty, the very helpful anonymous readers of the manuscript, and everyone at Oxford University Press.

Whatever the most up-to-date technology, the best way to find new fiction is at a really good bookshop that has interested and thoughtful staff, so I'd like to thank everyone at the wonderful Clapham Books for all their help and suggestions over many years. Independent bookshops need all the support they can get, so please use them if you can.

Most of all, I'd like to thank the students on my 'Ideas in Contemporary Fiction' course: I learned more than I taught.

List of illustrations

Chapter 1
Saying everything

Literature thinks.

Literature is where ideas are investigated, lived out, explored in all their messy complexity. Sometimes these ideas look quite simple: What if you fell in love with someone who seems quite unsuitable for you? What happens if there is a traitor in your spy network? Sometimes they might appear more complicated: How can I reconstruct my memory of an event I can't recall? Perhaps, too, 'think' is not the right word: 'think' is too limiting a description of the range of what a novel can do with ideas. In any event, the way literature thinks is bound up with what it's like to be us, to be human. Literature is how we make ourselves intelligible to ourselves. And contemporary fiction matters because it is how we work out who we are now, today.

I believe the novel is the best way of doing this. Of all the arts, the novel is the most thoughtful, the closest, the most personal. Unlike the visual arts or architecture or music or computer games, the novel uses only language. Nearly every one of us is an expert user of language and, more importantly, nearly everyone is an expert creator in language. Every day we use words to express ourselves and to tell stories, to make patterns out of our reality. We all share and thrive in language: we are much more intimate

with the novel's medium than we are with theatre or film.
Unlike much poetry or painting, fiction has narrative, sometimes
in complex ways. We share this with the novel, too, because each
of us, in the stories we tell every day, is a skilled author and weaver
of narrative. We can all judge a novel by the high and demanding
standards of our own use of words and stories and by our own
patterns of reality. Because it takes longer to read a novel than it
does to see a film or to listen to a piece of music and because
novels demand more time and energy, they are more immersive.
This is the origin of phrases like 'losing yourself in a book' or
'the book speaks to me', as if a novel was more than just ink on a
page or words on a screen. We *live in* novels more than in any
other art form, and after reading them, they stay with us
(an 'after-reading'). The novel is still the art form most deeply
and directly engaged with us.

More than this, the contemporary novel is the best way of
thinking about who we are now because fiction is also the freest
of all the arts. Despite many attempts to create one, there is no
real, watertight definition of fiction. It's not simply 'made up', it
doesn't just tell a story. Originally, 'definition' meant the setting
of bounds or limits: it's not at all clear what the limits of fiction
are, or indeed if there are any. The controversial French
philosopher Jacques Derrida, who thought and wrote a great
deal about this, described literature as a 'strange institution' and
argued that the 'institution of fiction...gives in principle the
power to say everything, to break free of the rules'. He defines
fiction as a form of writing that has no definition, no limits in
what it can say. The most important consequence of this is that
a novel can respond to any aspect of the world that the writer is
interested in, can be about anything, and can take any form or
forms it chooses. The world is multiple and complex: so is the
novel. There are no hard and fast rules for reading (or writing)
fiction. A novel might go absolutely anywhere or do anything.
This is the idea, this excitement, this freedom of the
contemporary novel, that underlies this book.

This unbound freedom of fiction in combination with the huge number of novels published every year (too many each year for any one person to read in a lifetime) also means that, in contemporary fiction, there can be no real experts in the conventional sense: who, anyway, could be an expert on flowing quicksilver that can go anywhere? But thinking about novels in this way, thinking about how they think, does offer ways of avoiding common pitfalls. For example, what a novel thinks is not the same as what an author thinks. Some book reviewers and journalists, perhaps inadvertently, suggest that we can only appreciate a novel in the context of a writer's life (and some writers play up to this). Often, this means that we pay attention to the correlation between two stories: the story of the novel (or a bad summary of the novel) and the story of the writer's life. Or, in the case of contemporary fiction, we can listen to the author her- or himself tell you what a book is about. Both of these mean that we no longer pay attention to the actual novel itself, which is surely why we were interested in the first place. One, very excusable, reason for this phenomenon is that it is actually hard to make out what 'knowing about' a novel actually means: knowing the plot? knowing what it means while knowing that it means very different things to very different people? knowing that it made you cry or smile? In the face of this uncertainty, turning to the story of an author's life or opinions gives a sense of security that some real fact is being told or some real 'knowing about' is happening. This seems to me quite wrong-headed. Knowing that a book makes you weep, or that it was boring, seems to me to be a fine subjective sort of knowledge. Knowing how it seems to fit into some bigger picture, finding its place in a larger constellation, seems to me to be a better, if more provisional, form of knowledge. And paying attention to its 'thinking', what a novel seems to be saying, seems to me to be the best form of knowing about contemporary fiction. But none of these is 'expertise' as the word is usually understood.

This freedom of the novel also makes the question of 'how we work out who we are' very demanding. 'We' is quite a complicated word, not least because it includes and excludes simultaneously. Who 'we' are, the communities of which each of us feels a part, is central to understanding the contemporary novel. The question is: who is the 'we' made intelligible by a novel's thinking? The novel used to be seen as a place where a national tradition revealed and reinforced a community, a 'we'. However, modern novels have become increasingly global, they cross and mix traditions and cultures, travel, and are translated. The idea of a national tradition of, say, the English or American or Kenyan novel has been bypassed by globalization. Optimistically, the 'post-national' novel might suggest that readers could learn about each other's differences, hopes, and fears and that our 'we' could be infinitely enlarged. 'We' might all become intelligible to each other. Pessimistically, some novels are ignored, misunderstood, or simply marketed as exotic novelties, and in the face of the whole world, our communities may become more defensive and less outgoing. Either way, the novel, like the human species, is now global and the form is still coming to terms with this deep and recent change.

A further symptom of this unboundedness and of the 'globalization' of the novel is that there is no real agreement about when the contemporary is. We know the contemporary ends in the present, but when does it start? Traditionally, literary periods take their dates from watershed historical moments. In Western Europe, for example, the period of the contemporary might begin in 1945. Yet, even within Europe, there are differences: in Spain, the contemporary might begin with the death of Franco in 1975; in Germany with the end of the Cold War in 1989 or reunification in 1990. Outside Europe things are very different again: contemporary might mean the end of the USSR in 1991 in Russia or independence from Britain in 1947 in India. Different communities have different senses of 'when' they are living, when the current moment began. More, the rapid historical and technological change through which we are living not only makes the past recede faster, it also weakens the very historical communities that define themselves by these sorts of dates, so perhaps watershed dates are not very helpful. In any case, it seems odd to mark a literary period with an 'extra-literary' event, however momentous. It takes time for historical events to move through into literature and for literature to make historical events intelligible. Instead, perhaps the 'contemporary' might mark the end of a previous literary age: the contemporary comes after modernism, perhaps, or postmodernism. Then again, did everywhere have 'modernism'? And what did that consist of? This book aims simply to cut the Gordian knot of this sort of debate and say that 'contemporary' means the last ten years or so. This doesn't prevent contemporary fiction dealing with the past, the present, or the future, as I will show, but it does mean that in ten years or so this book will be out of date. But evanescence is no bad thing for a book about the contemporary novel.

Chapter 2
Form, or, what's contemporary about contemporary fiction?

Form is everything. It is the secret of life.

Oscar Wilde

...if literature knows something, or knows of something, then we shall need at some stage to ask what literary forms know or know of.

Michael Wood

The French Russian experimental writer Nathalie Sarraute compared literature to a relay race, with a 'baton of innovation passing from one generation to another' (and the experimental British writer B. S. Johnson added rather unkindly that the problem was that the 'vast majority of British novelists had dropped the baton, stood still, turned back or not even realized that there is a race'). So it's fair to ask: where is the baton now? What is the next big thing, the next big movement? But this question is really less about what novels are *about* (as they are about us, in all our human complexity) as how they *work*. It's a question about what's at the core of any literary movement or moment: literary form, and how form is understood.

The underlying how

But if 'form' is the issue, what *is* form? Irritatingly, for writers, and *very* irritatingly for literary critics like me, there is no clear definition of what 'form' means, even though it is such an important concept. (Indeed, there are no clear definitions in literature: they are all leaky, vague, and should be abandoned when they are no longer useful. They are more like pointers drawing attention to an aspect of a work than a container to entrap it.) Form is of those simple-sounding words that turns out to be very complicated. Roughly, form is not *what* is written, but *how* something is written. Form describes not the content of a novel, but rather the ways in which a novel embodies or shapes that content, how a novel works. Form, and the decisions that form makes, is what makes a novel different from (or the same as, because novels can do anything they want) a history book or a newspaper (but these types of writing have their own form too). Form is the telling of the tale, and—as we can't separate the tale from the telling nor the dancer from the dance—that means that form is the core of the novel. Form is the writer's way of seeing and their way of telling. Form is what makes art artistic and literature literary.

I can imagine a creative writing exercise about form: retell this story as a detective thriller; as a romantic comedy; as a recipe book. Here the form would control how the story ended, what it meant. Form includes decisions about narration, too: tell these events from the protagonist's point of view or from a neutral all-knowing observer's point of view or as if you were the murderer and wanted to hide your crime. Things apart from plot are also decided by form: if the story is a comedy or a romance it's unlikely to dwell on the plight of the starving street children. Conversely, if it's a novel about the 'state of the nation' then the young lovers won't be the centre of attention and the street children will be. Form also shapes the choice of words, the length of sentences. Hard-boiled thrillers have short sentences. A clipped vocabulary. Sentences in academic texts, on the other hand, are long and drawn out, characterized by subclauses, usually but not always full of qualifications, and display a detailed complexity, certainly in their lexical and syntactic choices (their words and grammar).

Form also is at the core of change in art, and in literature. Artistic movements are first of all about form. When people talk about movements in literature (Romanticism, Modernism) they are talking not so much about the content of fiction, but rather the form: form is a way of seeing and telling, and we measure movements in how their telling has changed, how it has made us see or think about the world differently. So, when people ask, 'What's the next big thing?' in literature, they are not really asking 'What's the next big topic?' as if the answer could be the environment or terrorism. Instead, they are asking: how is the way this story is told going to challenge how we see and tell the world and ourselves?

But very often, although it is the very shaping of the novel, form is invisible. This sounds an odd thing to say but this invisibility stems from the origin of the novel as an art form, and with the cluster of ideas around what is called 'realism'. 'Realism', annoyingly, is also one of those words that sounds easy but, in fact, is very complex. 'Realist' does not just mean 'real' like the 'real world'. Novels have always told 'real world' stories about ordinary people doing ordinary things (falling in love, dying, eating) and they have also told extraordinary stories (making human monsters, giant suits of haunted armour, wizards on broomsticks): for realism, it isn't a matter of *content* of the story but of the *way* in which the story is told. Realism is a form that pretends to offer a window into a world through which one sees the events as if they were really happening, regardless of whether they are ordinary (falling in love) or extraordinary (flying on a broomstick). Realism is the dominant form of the novel. This is why so many novels can so easily be turned into films or television serials: the window is the screen. And yet, this is very strange.

Realism offers 'a window through which one sees a world' but, of course, in a novel, you don't 'see'. You read. Reading and interpreting are very complicated processes at which we have become so proficient that we almost no longer realize we are doing them.

When we read novels we take things for granted and we accept the *conventions* of realism. We read as if, for example, the characters in the novel are real people, that's why we feel, say, frightened for them, whether they are being threatened by poverty or a totalitarian police force. We read as if we expect one thing to follow another in the novel in a logical, cause-and-effect way, as if things have logical consequences. Importantly, from the first line of the first page, we read expecting an end to the story, expecting closure. Closure is what Frank Kermode, one of the leading literary critics of the 20th century, called the 'sense of an ending' and he argued that it was one of the most important and enduring features of fiction. It is the sense that a story is going to conclude, have the loose ends tied up, the bad ending badly, the good ending happily, and so on—having the story finished. Of course, in the world of the story some conventions might be different. We might accept that magic works and has a logic in one novel, for example, or that, in another, the world of the story is just like our world with the same streets and government ministers, where magic is just sleight of hand. But in a way, these are minor matters compared to the sense that we are 'seeing' these characters, and that they are real, that they are in a story that has closure. It is these realist conventions that we are very used to: indeed, we are so used to them that they have become invisible. We take realism in the novel for granted. Of course, realist fiction is never really utterly real: sometimes we find things simply very unlikely (the man who randomly rescued this one lost orphan in London turned out to be the orphan's *grandfather*? Oh, come on! Or, oh look, she *never* would really have fallen in love with *him*.). And more or less, all the books we read play games with us (Why did it mention that gun on the wall in Chapter 2? Will it turn out to be useful, I wonder?). But despite this, realism is the dominant form of the novel.

The baton

But there has always been a counter current to this dominance. In the 1700s, Laurence Sterne's *Tristram Shandy* played with page layouts, had long circumlocutions, uncertain characters, illogical plot development, and so on. At the end of the 19th century and the beginning of the 20th, writers like Henry James and Joseph Conrad wrote fiction which demanded more work of its readers to discover what was going on: the assured and often comforting narrative voices and final endings of Charles Dickens or George Eliot were missing, leaving a sense of confusion. The next generation of writers, James Joyce and Virginia Woolf and others, now clumped together as 'Modernist writers', questioned realism in much more dramatic ways, using different forms of writing and style in an attempt to get closer to a representation of consciousness. Famously Woolf wrote that that life 'is not a series of gig lamps symmetrically arranged; life is a luminous halo, a semi-transparent envelope surrounding us from the beginning of consciousness to the end'. That is, roughly speaking, Woolf was working out ways to resist the realist conventions of the novel in which one thing followed as a consequence of another in a linear chronology on the way to a (satisfying) narrative closure at the end. She wanted to resist this because, simply, modern life just isn't like that. Not only is closure hard to achieve in life (because the threads rarely all tie up), but our psyches seem to leap backwards and forwards in time, beset by memories of the past and hopes, fears, and expectations of the future in a complex and demanding world in which less and less seems certain.

The more experimental writers of the 1960s and 1970s developed these sorts of ideas. For example, B. S. Johnson wrote his novel *The Unfortunates* (1969) on cards, so that it could be shuffled and so read and reread in any order, and in this way rejected a linear and chronological narrative and a sense of closure. The novels of the experimental French writer Alain Robbe-Grillet followed geometric not chronological patterns. Meanwhile, writers like the German novelist Günter Grass and the Columbian writer Gabriel García Márquez were experimenting with magical realism, in which a traditional narrative, which looked like our (unmagical) world, was suddenly interrupted by the impossible, as if the enchantments of folk tales had broken into the more mundane world. In Grass's *The Tin Drum* (1959), for example, the child protagonist, Oskar, decides to stop growing up as a response to the rise of Nazism, and develops a superpowered scream that can damage people and buildings. These were all attempts to question or develop a form of the novel that was not, or not only, realist.

The last runner to pass on the baton, the immediate backdrop to the contemporary novel, however, is the literary movement known as postmodernism. This was the last generation's attempt to counter the realism typical of the novel. It's not easy to answer the question 'What is postmodernism?' quickly or accurately, because to answer it is to try to answer the question 'What was the mood of an age?', an issue on which no one will readily agree. The French philosopher Jean Francois Lyotard argued in 1979 that postmodernism was 'incredulity about metanarratives': that is, that 'we' (whoever we were) no longer believed in the great overarching stories which gave meaning to life: we no longer believed in the forward movement of human progress which made every advance seem like another step towards a better world, for example. In this, postmodernism was the apex of the process of disillusionment that Nietzsche saw when he declared the 'death of God' at the end of the 19th century. In contrast, the American critic Fredric Jameson saw postmodernism as the apogee of the meta-narrative of capitalism: if money dissolves all relationships into what they can be bought for, postmodernism is the point at which traditions themselves—'depth' he calls it—are destroyed by capitalism, and anything goes. But it's possible—while admitting that all categories are only suggestions—to see some of the outlines of postmodernism in the novel. Postmodernism certainly developed from the techniques of modernism and experimental fiction, and drew easily on magical realism and on the newer global reach of fiction, but perhaps its central characteristic was one of 'retelling': postmodern fiction retells in different ways what has been told before.

Most importantly, postmodern fiction retells its own telling. If realism wants to convince us, the readers, that the texts are windows through which we can see the fictional world, postmodernism wishes to banish that idea entirely. Postmodern fiction delights in stressing the fact that it is fiction, that it is made up. It does this in many ways: in playing games with the text or even with the print, in happily making an incoherent world in which, for example, magic works and then doesn't, or is seen as working only because the text is a fiction. Another very popular way to demonstrate this is to discuss the novel itself in the very act of writing: to be self-referential, in other words. Linda Hutcheon, an eminent critic of postmodernism, describes this as the novel's move from 'mimesis of product to mimesis of process', from the representation, that is, of a finished world to the representation of the process of representation itself. Salman Rushdie's *Midnight's Children* (1981), for example, describes its own telling and its own rhetorical tricks and strategies as it's going along.

Postmodern fiction also retells or reworks other writing, narratives or other art forms, often as pastiche. The British writer Angela Carter, for example, reused fairy stories to retell stories about sex and about gender, and in her novel *Nights at the Circus* (1984) she pastiches not only the Victorian gothic but also, for example, academic discussions of prisons. Postmodern fiction also often brings together high and low forms of culture, referencing Greek myths and popular cinema, pop music and opera, without any sense of this being a problem. This reusing also emerges in what critics call 'intertextuality', the ways in which one literary text reuses or refers to another: for example, Jane Smiley's novel *A Thousand Acres* (1991), set in a farming community in Iowa, retells *King Lear*.

If realist fiction often 'tells' the reader what to think, postmodern fiction puts the emphasis on the work of interpretation, forcing the reader to 'retell' to themselves what happens. Retelling in this case is a form of interpretation. A famous example of this is

Thomas Pynchon's *The Crying of Lot 49* (1966), a novel, a friend of mine remarked, that could have been written to teach postmodernism (a joke, but also a warning about the ways in which academics create 'movements' and 'typical novels'). At the core of the book is the pursuit of a possibly fictional secret society, and the reader is left to decide if there is such a society, or if the protagonist is mad, or if she is simply being set up, or if the whole thing is a joke. But this emphasis on interpretation, rather than a straightforward story with a conclusion and a moral, has a profounder meaning. By making the novel more demanding and complex to understand, it is refusing a simplistic closure or ending, and asks more of the reader: the reader is, indeed, centrally involved in deciding what the novel might mean. Closure is a way of finishing, of closing down an idea or an argument: to reject closure is to be interested in opening arguments up, in having more to say.

This refusal of closure goes hand in hand with an often ignored characteristic of postmodern fiction. While appearing to be playful, and obviously fictional, many postmodern novels are often deeply involved in politics and ethics. Toni Morrison's wonderful novel *Beloved* (1987) reuses a horrifying true story from the 1870s, about a recently freed African-American woman who murdered her own child. *Beloved* makes an important intervention into American cultural memory and political life by demonstrating that the psychological and cultural impact of slavery cannot easily be dismissed or bypassed. It gives a voice to the suffering of the past. Similarly, *Foe* (1986), by the South African novelist J. M. Coetzee, retells the story of Robinson Crusoe from the point of view of Crusoe's wife, 'expunged' (in this fiction) from the original story. Through the character of Friday, it not only obliquely criticizes the evil system of apartheid, then extant in South Africa, and the ways in which people are censored, but also warns about the corrupting dangers of speaking for others for whom one has no warrant. This form of ethical and political retelling, often about people who have been marginalized by the historical record or by the dominant 'closed' stories, is central to much postmodern fiction.

These roughly sketched characteristics (stressing the fact that a novel is a text and not a 'real' thing, reusing other forms of writing, stressing the reader's role in interpreting the text, rejecting closure, and including the voices of those who were often excluded from the mainstream of history and representation) also illustrate the idea that most postmodern fiction shares: a belief that 'narrative' itself is one of the most powerful forces there is. Stories, it implies, and the culture of stories, shape us more than we know and to change the stories is to change the world. This is a very reassuring belief for novelists and storytellers (and critics and journalists) as it seems to empower words over the more brute forces of existence.

That was then, this is . . .

If postmodernism was the dominant mode in which realism was challenged in the novel in the 1980s and 1990s, how has it been challenged or developed by writers in contemporary fiction? Of course, writers have explored different topics or taken different angles but the question here is about change in the form of the novel. It may be that in the huge range of contemporary fiction, it's now impossible to draw out a movement. However, I think it's possible to identify some trends.

First, there is retreat from the extreme playfulness of postmodernism and the emphasis on textuality and on difficulty. But, crucially, this retreat is not a simple reaction against and rejection of all the techniques of postmodernism, but rather a gentler, more accessible version of them, with a strong interest in telling a story. For example, British novelist David Mitchell's novel *Cloud Atlas* (2004) is made up of interlocking stories, one within the other. One of its main sources of inspiration is the 'classic of postmodernism', *If on a Winter's Night a Traveller*

(1979), by the Italian writer Italo Calvino. In Calvino's novel, different stories follow each other and none of the stories is finished: there is no end, no closure. In contrast, in Mitchell's novel, the stories, while interrupted in turn, *are* finished, do end. Similarly, the American novelist Jonathan Safran Foer plays textual games in his much celebrated first novel *Everything Is Illuminated* (2002): things are blotted out, there is pastiche of other writers (including the Nobel Laureate Isaac Bashevis Singer), repetition of phrases over several pages, and indeed some of the events are purposively obscured through an intricate and tricky use of the chronology in the novel (a final letter, the last moment of the novel chronologically, is quite a way from the end of the novel by pages). These are postmodern-style tricks here put at the use of a very strong narrative thread. Even the American writer Jonathan Frantzen, who is more 'strictly' realist, employs some typographical and literary games in *The Corrections* (2001) and pastiche and intertextuality in his more recent *Freedom* (2010). Still, if the word 'post-postmodernism' wasn't too silly in itself, it wouldn't be accurate precisely because, while these writers have clearly learned a great deal from the experimentalism of postmodernism and its forebears, they have integrated it, domesticated it, and returned some way to the more traditional forms of the novel.

There seems to me to be an emblematic moment which describes retreat from postmodernism in Mitchell's charming (and less showy) novel *Black Swan Green*. The protagonist, a monolingual thirteen-year-old school boy in provincial England, has encountered a glamorous Belgian expat, Madame Crommelynck, who has introduced him, suddenly, to a much wider and more exciting culture than his own, full of aesthetic experimentation. He begins to write poetry, to make his way painfully through Alain-Fournier's *Le Grand Meaulnes* (1913) in French ('Translations are incourteous between Europeans,' proclaims Crommelynck). But suddenly, after this opening of his horizons, Madame Crommelynck is arrested for fraud or embezzlement and extradited to Germany. She disappears and so does this moment of opening to a greater (European) complexity. The narrator returns then to less tricky ways of writing. And there's a corresponding moment in Mitchell's *Cloud Atlas*, too, where a conservative-minded publisher dismissively says that as 'an experienced editor I disapprove of backflashes, foreshadowings and tricksy devices, they belong in the 1980s with MAs in Postmodernism and Chaos Theory'. Despite this reaction to broader vistas of the mind and of art, both the more realist *Black Swan Green* and the publisher's tale in *Cloud Atlas* bear some of the traces of 'high postmodernism'.

Second, there is a return to a sort of modernism. Drawing on the heritage of Woolf, Joyce, and Beckett, and on the experimental fiction of the next generation, B. S. Johnson, Christine Brooke-Rose, and Anne Quinn, some writers find in these the resources to continue to develop fiction. The critic Laura Marcus draws attention to the return of the 'one day' novel—the framing conceit of *Mrs Dalloway* (1925) and *Ulysses* (1922)—in which a whole life, a whole world, is condensed into a day. Ian McEwan's *Saturday* (2005) does this, as does Don DeLillo's *Cosmopolis* (2003). But perhaps another aspect of this is the 'multi-strand' novel, influenced again by Woolf, but by *The Waves* (1931), and by Joyce. Ali Smith's brilliant *The Accidental* (2005) is of this sort. It begins during a rather stress-filled family holiday in Norfolk. The family all have something to hide: the mother, Eve, a novelist who has been writing novels based on extrapolating the events of real people's lives from the Second Word War, is blocked; the stepfather, Michael, has been having affairs with his students; Magnus, the son, has been tangentially involved in a terrible bullying incident at school; Astrid, the precocious daughter, is unhappy and obsessed with taking photographs. Into this situation wanders a strange young woman, Amber, who befriends each of them and works as a catalyst for the plot. But the events are only as important as the multiple strands and styles. The narrative proceeds through the very different consciousnesses of the characters, interweaving in a non-linear way, shifting and playing games with the chronology. More than this, the styles of the novel echo the characters in a non-realist and modernist way. One part is written (as a chapter of *Ulysses* is) in questions and answers, as Eve interrogates her writer's block; another, as Michael agonizes over his sex life, uses different modes of English love poetry from a 'sonnet sequence(y)' section through an e.e.cummings imitation page, through a Larkinesque rant, and into a parody of Byron's *Don Juan*. What's 'really happening' becomes hard to tell as the events are so filtered through each of the characters. Similarly, Hari Kunzru's *Gods without Men* (2011) is about a strange outcrop of rocks in the south-western United States that may, or may not, have connections with divine or alien presences: again, in a typically modernist way, the 'truth' of this is never made clear. Rather, in a multistranded narrative we are given different historical moments in which these rocks feature: a 17th-century monk's diary, an ethnologist in the 1920s, a UFO hunter in the 1950s, and a late 1960s space love cult. The largest thread concerns a couple whose autistic child disappears near the rocks. In none of these cases—nor in the book as a whole—is there a full 'closure': the stories, filtered through the consciousness of each protagonist, have uncertain, disturbing endings. Again, as in modernist fiction, the reader has to decide what happened, to come to their own conclusions.

A third and perhaps equally important new wave in contemporary fiction is a turn away from fiction as it had been understood altogether. In his extraordinary *Reality Hunger: A Manifesto*, made up mostly from quotations from other writers and thinkers but crafted into a collage-like argument, the American novelist and critic David Shields writes that there is an 'organic and as-yet-unstated' artistic movement forming around writers and artists who are 'breaking larger and larger chunks of "reality" into their works':

What are its key components? A deliberate unartiness: 'raw' material, seemingly unprocessed, unfiltered, uncensored, and unprofessional...Randomness, openness to accident and serendipity, spontaneity; artistic risk, emotional urgency and intensity, reader/viewer participation: an overly literal tone, as if a reporter were viewing a strange culture; plasticity of form, pointillism; criticism as autobiography; self-reflexivity, self-ethnography, anthropological autobiography; a blurring (to the point of invisibility) of any distinction between fiction and nonfiction: the lure and bur of the real.

Shields, or perhaps his collage-argument ('collargument', perhaps), points out that the 'etymology of fiction is from *fingere*...meaning to "shape, fashion, form, or mould". Any verbal account is a fashioning and shaping of events.' Fiction does not first mean 'made up'. But Shields is not saying that writing could be just a simple representation of the world. 'Collaging' the American novelist and memoirist Vivian Gornick, from her book on writing memoirs, *The Situation and the Story* (2001), he argues that what 'happened to the writer isn't what matters; what matters is the larger sense that the writer is able to make of what happened. For that, the power of a writing imagination is required.' Nor is Shields being naive about the strong pull of authenticity. The German philosopher Theodore Adorno wrote an attack on the idea of authenticity, pointing out precisely how the claim that something is 'authentic' or real is just another form of jargon, a clever form of fakeness. The insistence on things 'being real' is one of the most unreal things there is (as in the old joke that the best politicians fake sincerity). Shields is also aware that the line between fiction and non-fiction has always been blurred. The American writer Truman Capote's second most famous work is a 'non-fiction novel', *In Cold Blood* (1966). The experiences of the Polish-British writer Joseph Conrad in the Congo, as his diary, letters, and biography show, are worked into the celebrated novella 'Heart of Darkness' (1902). But, Shields suggests, not only are 'biography and autobiography...the lifeblood of art right now' but there is a whole cultural turn towards an idea of reality. He is interested in the contemporary transmutation of 'the real' into—I'm putting scare quotes around the word now because it doesn't mean what it did—'fiction'.

Outside the world of contemporary writing this transmutation of 'the real' into 'fiction' does seem to be the case. There are countless reality TV shows, some of which clearly state that they are a blurring of the line between 'reality' and 'fiction' (one example says that it is 'real people in modified situations, saying unscripted lines but in a structured way'). There has been a rise in verbatim theatre in which the script is taken from other sources (government enquiries, court cases, and so on). Artists like Tracey Emin take experiences and the concrete material from their own lives, not as the inspiration of art but as the artwork itself (a recent Emin exhibition, for example, featured the last packet of cigarettes bought by her uncle before he died in a car crash). In writing, too, there has also been a turn to 'reality'. Works of history and biography are terribly popular, which itself speaks of 'reality hunger'. These are not only the stories of major battles, presidents, or princesses. Kate Summerscale's *The Suspicions of Mr Whicher* (2008) is the history of a murder in 1860, now forgotten, retold using all the rhetoric of a detective novel. Similarly, her book about a scandalous Victorian divorce, *Mrs Robinson's Disgrace* (2012), reads like a sensational, almost romantic, novel. Shields is right, I think, that in contemporary fiction there has been a turn to the 'real'. Shields himself is influenced by two of the most significant writers of contemporary fiction, writers whose influence on form seeps through much that has been written in the last ten years. Both these writers display some of the characteristics that Shields identifies.

The first of these two is W. G. Sebald. Born in 1944 in Germany, Sebald lived and worked in the UK: he was killed in a car crash in 2001. In an astonishing series of complex and elegiac works, of which only the last, *Austerlitz* (2001), is a (more or less)

Quid Quincunce speciosius, qui, inquam cunqз partem spectaueris, rectus est: Quintilian://

1. Thomas Browne's 'Quincunx', reproduced from W. G. Sebald's *The Rings of Saturn*: a way of suggesting The interrelations between events

straightforward novel, Sebald seemed to pioneer a new form of writing. *The Rings of Saturn* (1995 in German, 1998 in English) describes, in the first person, a walking tour around Suffolk, a tour which gave the narrator not only a sense of freedom but also a sense of 'paralysing horror' when 'confronted with the traces of destruction, reaching far back into the past, that were evidence even in that remote place' which in turn led to his hospitalization. The idea that underlies the book comes from the 17th-century writer Thomas Browne (1605–82): Browne identified everywhere in nature what he called the 'quincunx', an interlacing connective pattern which links everything in nature together. (Browne himself, who wrote not quite natural science, not quite philosophy, not quite history, not quite religious works, but texts that pertained to all of these, serves as a model for Sebald, too.) For the protagonist of Sebald's text, the things he sees link with threads of history to everything else, and all link to terrible atrocities or melancholic decay. An abandoned iron bridge over the river Blyth has a narrow-gauge railway and the train that used to run over it was originally made for the emperor of China. It was never sent to China because of the Taiping Rebellion and the terrible siege of Nanking: the 'bloody horror in China at that time went beyond all imagining'. A chance conversation about sugar beet reminds the narrator that people made rich by the sugar trade (and so by slavery) often invested in art (the Tates in the UK, for example); in turn this leads to a visit to an abandoned sugar beet plantation, the house of which was destroyed by a V1 bomb during the Second World War. This house was, in turn, the seat of the melancholic poet and translator Edward Fitzgerald, who presided over the decline of the estate. The book's literary 'surface' is also broken—as all Sebald's works are—by photographs. These are black and white, bleak, and clearly add to the 'reality effect' of the work. That said, while some are clearly of the things they describe, the provenance and accuracy of some are not clear at all: again, the many pictures themselves question the relationship between fiction and the real. The title of the book comes from the theory that the beautiful rings of the planet Saturn are the fragmented remains of a destroyed former moon: beauty and destruction linked together. While the historical (and often incidental) stories of death and decay fascinate, they also distract the reader from the narrator. But if these continual stories of destruction are a mirror of the narrator's mind, the book is also the story of a breakdown told in that mirror. It becomes quite impossible to say whether this is fact or fiction.

As a contrast to this very melancholic European writing, while still expressing 'reality hunger', is the exuberance of the American writer David Eggers. His first novel is *A Heartbreaking Work of Staggering Genius* (2000). Ostensibly the story of his parents' death and of how he raised his younger brother, the book is packed with jokes and plays with the very idea of the novel. The weirdness of the book is clear from the start, from before the start, actually: on the imprint page which details the publisher's information, the Library of Congress data, and so on, Eggers has toyed with the layout and the conventional legal disclaimers. He writes:

> This is a work of fiction, only in that in many cases, the author could not remember the exact words said by certain people, and exact descriptions of certain things, so had to fill in gaps as best he could. Otherwise, all characters and incidents and dialogue are real, are not products of the author's imagination, because at the time of this writing, the author had no imagination whatsoever for those sorts of things, and could not conceive of *making up* a story or characters—it felt like driving a car in a clown suit—especially when there was so much to say about his own, true, sorry and inspirational story, the actual people that that he has known, and of course the many twists and turns of his own thrilling and complex mind. Any resemblance to persons living or dead should be plainly apparent to them and those who know them, especially if the author has been kind enough to have provided their real names and, in some cases, their phone numbers. All events described herein actually happened, though on occasion the author has taken certain, very small, liberties with chronology, because that is his right as an American.

Many of the themes and ideas of the book, in addition to its playfulness, are apparent here. The blurring of the conventional line between reality and fiction (the author had to 'fill in gaps', the liberties with the chronology); the drive to even more reality (the phone numbers) as at the same time reality recedes; the playing with conventions (with the usual 'no resemblance to persons living or dead' rhetoric); the self-reflective discussion of the very nature of writing fiction ('driving a car in a clown suit'); the delicate balancing on the line between self-aggrandizement and the ironic deflation of that same self-aggrandizement ('true, sorry and inspirational story', 'his own thrilling and complex mind' 'because that is his right as an American'). This last characteristic also reflects an ambiguity about the moral sense of the book. In some ways, *A Heartbreaking Work of Staggering Genius* is a moral book interested in correct behaviour: it can be judgemental, for example. But at the same time, it questions this continually with gentle irony and humour. Indeed, the book is funny as well as sad: it begins with amusing 'Rules and Suggestions for Enjoyment of this book'. Rather like some of the books I discussed earlier, this couldn't have been written without the experimentalism and explorations of postmodern fiction. Like those books it has a very strong narrative thread but unlike them, it is doing something more than just that. In its commitment to a sense of the real, and its interrogation of just that commitment, it is embodying just what Shields is trying to analyse.

Endings?

To ask 'Where is contemporary fiction today?' then, is to ask about how writers explore the form of the novel. Of course, the majority of novels published are realist, but there seem to be, as I've suggested, three sorts of areas of challenge to this realism special to the last ten years or so. The first is a retreat from the wilder edges of postmodernism towards a stronger sense of narrative. This retreat, however, has not forgotten the lessons of postmodern fiction: these texts are still playful, still complex over issues like textuality and closure. The second is a renewed interest in techniques of high modernism, associated with Woolf and Joyce. The third involves the demolition of the barriers between the realms of fiction and non-fiction writing.

All three of these seem to have a nuanced approach to the central issue of closure. Neither quite revelling in the sense of an ending, as the more traditional form of the novel does, nor rejecting the idea of closure altogether, they do draw towards an end but leave much undecided or uncertain. This is true even of 'reality' art. David Shields again: as 'work gets more autobiographical, more intimate, more confessional, more embarrassing, it breaks into fragments. Our lives aren't pre-packaged along narrative lines and, therefore, by its very nature, reality-based art—under-processed, under-produced—splinters and explodes.' It's true, though, of the other more clearly fictional novels. The endings of Ali Smith are not clear-cut, but require thought and work on the part of the reader. These trends seem to suggest that there's no longer simply one line of innovation, one set of runners passing on a baton, but that a wider and more complex race is still being run.

Chapter 3
Genre

Genre is a minimum security prison.

David Shields

Genre is one of the most important ideas in contemporary fiction. It is also an idea in complete disarray. In one area, genres are in total flux: novels mix and blur genres, combining, for example, the historical novel with the detective thriller, or blending science fiction into a novel about the concrete present day. In another, the boundaries of genre are rigidly enforced by publishers, academics, booksellers, and journalists: novels are branded by genre as clearly as cleaning products, so that the book buyer always knows 'what's inside the tin'. A further symptom of this disarray lies in the unending proliferation of names of genres and subgenres for novels, as if a need to classify writing has created an army of literary carpenters, frantically manufacturing pigeonholes in which to fit new novels. The aim of this chapter is to explore these oddly opposing and confused ideas about of genre, but to do this, I'm going to go back to the peculiar definition of literature I gave in the Introduction.

... a strange institution

Ideas about genre are ideas about the institution of literature. Earlier, I cited Jacques Derrida, who suggested that literature was

2. Literature, an enormous institution: an Amazon warehouse

a 'strange institution' that allows one 'to say everything' and it's the first bit of this I want to focus on now. It's easy to think of institutions as buildings and organizations (universities are institutions, as are parliaments) but institutions are also cultural practices: people talk of the 'institution' of marriage, for example. As cultural practices, they are made up in part of material things and in part of the ideas we have and act on in relation to them. More than this, as cultural practices they have a history that can be traced and written.

Literature is certainly an institution. Indeed, contemporary fiction—one large part of this—is an *enormous* institution. It is a huge (*huge!*), multi-billion dollar business. It involves all sorts of different people in an interwoven fabric. Perhaps most importantly, there are millions upon millions of readers, and thousands of writers. But there is also a panoply of other people involved: publishers, publicists, festival organizers; printers and makers of e-reading devices; booksellers; literary agents to help (or hinder) the business; journalists who fill the book pages; bloggers who explore and argue online; librarians; fans and fan communities; students, teachers, and researchers at school and university. Each of these has a different relationship to the strange institution. For some, it's a business. Some journalists, for example, aren't really interested in what a book is like but who is hot, what is selling, who's talking to whom at the Frankfurt Book Fair each autumn (institution-as-business). Some academics are interested in what the books mean and what they can tell us about ourselves (institution-as-research). And students, while studying literature because they love it, also want to get good marks in their exams (institution-as-evaluation). Indeed, where the institution of literature has met education, it has created a whole world of teaching and understanding itself, which has its own complex history and internal stories and conflicts. In the syllabus for his literary interpretation class in 2005, the American writer David Foster Wallace (1962–2008) gave a good general introduction to how the institution of literature meets the institution of education by talking about 'critical appreciation'. This means:

> having smart, sophisticated reasons for liking whatever literature you like, and being able to articulate those reasons for other people, especially in writing. Vital for critical appreciation is the ability to 'interpret' a piece of literature, which basically means coming up with a cogent, interesting account of what a piece of lit means, what its trying to do to/for the reader, what technical choices the author's made in order to achieve the effects she wants and so on. As you can probably anticipate, the whole thing gets very complicated and abstract and hard, which is one reason why entire college departments are devoted to studying and interpreting literature.

And, I suspect, most readers are not that interested in either the 'business side' of the institution or the more recondite arguments of researchers and really only want to read, enjoy, and think about the books. Contemporary fiction really is a 'strange institution', a global one which almost has no idea that it *is* an institution, involving many millions of people, with many different understandings of what the institution is about.

However, one of the most interesting and most important parts of any institution is the mechanism by which the past history and traditions of the institution meet the present. In this 'strange institution' of literature, one of the most important ways this happens is called genre.

At first, genre, which basically just means 'type', looks relatively innocuous. In the case of contemporary fiction, it looks as if it's simply the 'pigeonhole' into which different sorts of novels are placed: science fiction, 'chicklit', historical fiction, thrillers, and so on. Bookshops and libraries need to know which shelves to place books on; book jacket designers need to know what to put on the cover (you can *always* judge a contemporary novel book by its cover: indeed, there is huge sub-industry just devoted to making this possible); teachers need to know where books go. It's almost as if everyone involved in the strange institution is keen to fit books into neat categories. This is nothing new, really: Aristotle's *Poetics* (c.335 BCE) is an account of the characteristics of the different types of drama and poetry. Sir Philip Sidney produced a list which classed poetry by type: epic, lyric, comic, satiric, elegiac, amatory. But this urge to classify fiction is itself a symptom of two more important aspects of the idea of genre that, in contemporary fiction, are in a tense relationship to each other. Genre is also utterly crucial to the idea of literary creation and to the idea of literary value.

Genre and literary creation

Genre isn't just where novels get shelved, it's also absolutely central to the creation of novels. Genres mark out, or name, what I will call 'lines of descent'. These lines are a bit like family trees and are central to the writing and to the reading of contemporary fiction. No work is created from nothing, and each writer, in creating, has in his or her mind the novels he or she has read. The great Argentinean writer Jorge Luis Borges, influenced by T. S. Eliot's seminal essay 'Tradition and the Individual Talent', wrote that 'every writer creates his own precursors' (and added that this 'modifies our conception of the past, as it will modify the future'). What this means is that writers choose what sort of novels to write by taking on ideas, plots, concepts, tricks of style, and approaches from writers they like and rejecting those they don't. They imitate and avoid. They choose their 'lines of descent' and often talk about the 'traditions' of writing that they draw on. Great writers are also great readers and are usually fascinating and insightful on the novelists that have influenced and shaped their work—their lines of descent. Previous novels and types of novels from all ages shape any piece of contemporary writing.

This means that literary history might be thought of as a sort of ongoing, interwoven conversation between writers and through self-chosen traditions. But these traditions are like many currents in a river: here one current is more powerful, here another, here two currents mix and cause turbulence: and a writer, rather than being set in a fixed, frozen block, like a glacier (she is a 'modernist'; he writes 'thrillers'), can take from each or any current. Some of these currents might be older (a realist tradition, for example) and from them something new might be wrested and developed (or not): or a writer might mix currents. In this way, writers (like all artists) are not only creators of art but also preservers of traditions of writing: they create new works and keep older currents going. These traditions, these streams coming through time, are called genres.

But more than this, these currents through time, these lines of descent control how we read and understand novels: they set our hopes and expectations. The American humorist James Thurber has a fantastic short story, 'The Macbeth Murder Mystery', in which a woman buys *Macbeth*, thinking it's a detective thriller in the style of Agatha Christie ('I don't see why the Penguin-books people had to get out Shakespeare plays in the same size and everything as the detective stories…Anyway, I got real comfy in bed that night and all ready to read a good mystery story and here I had *The Tragedy of Macbeth*—a book for high-school students.'). She whispers to the narrator of the story that:

I don't think for a moment that Macbeth did it...I don't think the Macbeth woman was mixed up in it, either. You suspect them the most, of course, but those are the ones that are never guilty—or shouldn't be, anyway...It would spoil everything if you could figure out right away who did it. Shakespeare was too smart for that. I've read that people never have figured out *Hamlet*, so it isn't likely Shakespeare would have made *Macbeth* as simple as it seems.

She is reading the play as if it were a different genre, and so, quite rightly, comes to different conclusions about who the murderers are. These expectations shape all our reading: it's impossible—or astonishingly rare, at any rate—I think, to begin reading a book with no preconceptions at all.

This sense of genre seems to me to be not only quite important, but also rather liberating: genre is that which enables people to shape their thoughts, feelings, ideas, and interests both as writers and as readers. But it runs up against another central idea in contemporary fiction.

Genre and literary value

The reasons that Aristotle, Sidney, and many others made typologies of literature is that genre has been intimately connected to ideas about *literary value*, to the ideas about how 'good' a work of literature is. Of course, each of us likes some novels more than others and we think that some are better than others, or more valuable. However, through the late 19th and 20th centuries, and largely because of the ways in which the study of English literature became ensconced in universities and schools, the idea arose that some works of fiction just were better and more valuable than others. Perhaps the central figures in creating this idea, certainly in the UK, were the critics F. R. and Q. D. Leavis. They and others created or argued for a 'great tradition' of fiction that had more 'life' than others. 'Life', for the Leavises, was a special term, not something that could be defined but that embodied

what was great about great literature. The 'great tradition' of
fiction made up what was called a *canon* of serious fiction: these
novels were more authentic, had more 'life', than others. (The
word and idea of the 'canon' was taken, perhaps not intentionally,
from disputes in the early Christian Church about which religious
writings were agreed to reveal the authentic truth and were thus
'canonical'. Similarly, to be in the canon of great fiction, novels
were thought to embody life or authenticity.) In contrast, novels
that were not serious or full of 'life' were not canonical. So, for
example, fiction about the past (historical novels), about
detectives, spies, and murders (thrillers), or about the impact of
new or imagined technologies (science fiction) became known as
'genre fiction' to distinguish it from proper 'literary fiction'.
However—and this was one thing that worried the Leavises and
others in the United States and the UK—'genre fiction' remained
the very most popular form of the novel. More people read
thrillers or romances or historical novels or science fiction than
literary fiction. Yet, since 'genre fiction' was not proper 'literary
fiction', no matter how well written it was, or how it addressed
important issues (after all, you might learn a lot about a society
from the stories it tells about those who enforce the rule of law),
it was regarded as an inferior form of writing. Genre—not the
quality of writing—became a way of judging literary value.

More than this, the same process of 'canonization' of literature
was often used to exclude writing from places outside Europe
and North America, or that didn't address 'serious issues':
writing by women was often passed over, for example. If a novel
was not thought to embody what was, say, 'truly American' or
perhaps 'quintessentially English', it was excluded from these
national canons. Of course, the books that were canonical
became the ones taught on curriculums in schools and
universities, further occluding genre fiction and 'inauthentic'
fiction, and further reinforcing the very ideas which created the
canon and reduced some fiction to the inferior category of 'genre
fiction'.

31

However, in the second half of the 20th century, there was a ferocious backlash against this attitude. The division of fiction into 'serious' or 'literary' fiction and 'genre' fiction looked snobbish, didn't seem to match people's experience of literature and their creation of their own personal canon of books they loved and treasured. Worse, it looked even anti-democratic. Why should certain books be excluded? What were the reasons for exclusion? In 1989, the Nobel Laureate Toni Morrison wrote that canon building 'is empire building. Canon defence is national defence. Canon debate, whatever the terrain, nature and range (of criticism, of history, of the history of knowledge, of the definition of language, the universality of aesthetic principles, the sociology of art, the humanist imagination) is the clash of cultures. And all the interests are vested.' Moreover, of course, for those reading to discover things about the world, there was as much sociological interest in a thriller as in a piece of 'serious' fiction. This backlash also went hand in hand with a more complex and deeper change in the whole idea of literary value. Earlier, it seemed almost as if there was a set of (admittedly vague) criteria of value by which literary texts could be judged (for the Leavises it was 'life'), implicitly acknowledged and enforced by teachers, academics, and journalists. Now it seemed that a sense of shared value had vanished. This backlash went on more in the universities than in the wider public world but by the beginning of the 21st century, even newspapers, for example, have stopped acting as if there is a divide between 'serious' and 'genre' fiction. The question of value, of whether a novel is well written or interesting, seemed to have disappeared.

Contemporary fiction and genre

However, I think contemporary fiction is now at another turning point. As I have suggested, the overall snobbery about the inferiority of 'genre fiction' to 'literary fiction' has declined. One paradoxical consequence of this has been the way in which genre has become more rigidly enforced in the production and reception of novels. Rather than fiction being a river in which different currents run, sometimes separate and sometimes mingling, it is as if the different currents have now become separated rivers winding through different courses. There are some—few—writers who creatively mix genres and traditions (there are examples later in this book) but the separation of fiction into genres seems increasingly powerful. An effect of this is to make all works of fiction seem as if they are genres. Literary fiction is often seen as a genre in itself: a genre that might, for example, be discussed as 'Booker' fiction, after the leading UK prize for literary fiction. But for all its origins in a democratic and anti-snobbish feeling, I think that this situation has a very worrying consequence.

I think it risks betraying what literature can do.

The idea with which I began argued that literature is a 'strange institution' that allows one 'to say everything'. Literature allows one to say everything, to say anything. Contrast literature—or, more specifically, fiction—with other forms of writing. A work of history is a form of writing with strict (though negotiable) rules: it must refer to external documents (usually by footnotes or endnotes); it tells a sort of narrative about a past event; it's usually in the third person (a first-person history is a memoir), and so on. A work of philosophy should (usually, but not always) put forward rational arguments. A cookbook, whatever else it has, must have recipes: a cookbook with no recipes is not a cookbook. But a work of fiction can have all these things, or none of them. A work of fiction can say anything. (This freedom makes people uneasy.)

But a work of genre fiction has limits and rules. Thrillers have adventures; detective stories have detectives (usually) and certainly detection; science fiction throws a 'new thing' (robots, space travel) into the world and sees what that does; romances have love and its vicissitudes. These limits are why David Shields writes that genre 'is a minimum security prison'.

But what limits does 'serious fiction' have? If it can say anything, do anything, in writing, then, surely, it has no limits.

This question can be looked at in more detail through an example using one of the most popular and interesting 'genres', science fiction. A novel that can be easily seen as science fiction can also be serious fiction (as Orwell's *1984* is, for example). Indeed, in 2005, Kazuo Ishiguro's novel *Never Let Me Go* was shortlisted for both the UK's serious fiction prize, the Man Booker, and for the UK's science fiction prize, the Arthur C. Clarke Award, because it featured a staple of science fiction, the idea of clones. But, in contrast, a serious literary fiction—with absolutely no clones or robots or spaceships or time travellers or anything typical of a science fiction novel—would not be shortlisted for a 'Science Fiction' prize precisely because it has no clones or robots or spaceships or time travellers or so on. There is a revealing 'non-reciprocity' there.

Science fiction is commonly defined as a genre that, at root, deals with the impact of technology (although, as I said, all definitions about literature are pretty ropey and should be abandoned as soon as they stop being useful). Science fiction is fiction into which a 'novum', a new thing, has been introduced into the world: faster-than-light travel, robots, hair that photosynthesizes, aliens from Mars, and so on. It then explores the impact of this 'novum' on society and the individual. However, people interested in science fiction often cite an idea from the famous British science fiction writer, Arthur C. Clarke, one of his 'laws': 'any sufficiently advanced technology is indistinguishable from magic'. This sounds like a cliché from the early 20th-century fiction Clarke would have read as a boy, abstracted from one of those colonial stories in which Europeans amaze 'natives' with some piece of technology (as if the 'natives' couldn't figure out that firing a gun is a bit like throwing a stone). It also says something unexpected about much science fiction, too. It implies that fiction about a sufficiently advanced technology is indistinguishable from fiction about magic. The 'novum' serves simply as a hook for an exciting story, just as 'magic' did in medieval romances or a prince being transformed into a frog by a witch does in a fairy tale. These 'new things', then, are not really technology but really equivalent to magic and serve only as a way of allowing an enjoyable generic adventure romp to occur. Faster-than-light travel simply enables people to meet strange new creatures and kill them heroically, for example. This means that, really, many of these sorts of novels aren't an engagement with technology, with the future, but an engagement with a modern vision of magic, and so simply a form of the genre of adventure fiction. There's nothing wrong with adventure stories, of course, but they are limited by their generic rules. They can't 'say everything'.

Science fiction, too, has become its own 'river': it has its own traditions, history, and development. Books write back to books on the same themes. H. G. Wells's evil Martians are 'replied' to by Ray Bradbury's mysterious ones, and in Kim Stanley Robinson's Mars trilogy, *Red Mars* (1993), *Green Mars* (1994), and *Blue Mars* (1996), the humans themselves become the destructive invaders, become Martians. The more a genre becomes its own tradition, the more it refers to itself, the more of a 'minimum security prison' it becomes. That is, even science fiction that aims to be more than an adventure story and to reflect back our ideas about ourselves to ourselves (as satire, for example) has limitations created by genre. Science fiction is the future told with rules from the present: both the future and the novel really reject the very possibility of rules. Paradoxically, this means that science fiction is most science (a 'novum') fiction (a novel, that can say anything) when it's not science fiction. Indeed, some writers such as Margaret Atwood invoke the name 'speculative fiction' to escape just this.

Genre is not made up by awards, but this illustrates a key idea about 'genre' fiction. If fiction can say anything, then genre fiction is *limited*. This is not to say it is bad or good, or better or less well written, but to say that unlike literary fiction that can be about anything, genre fiction is *restricted*. Ironically, it is restricted by precisely those things that people like about it. (Conversely, a science fiction novel *without one aspect* of science fiction is simply...a novel.)

There is then, 'open', unrestricted fiction and 'closed', restricted fiction. 'Open' fiction is what used to be called literary fiction, able to cover anything, in any form. 'Closed' fiction is what used to be called 'genre fiction', shaped by its own self-chosen restrictions. This is absolutely not to say that 'restricted' fiction, genre fiction, is badly written, badly plotted, or less valuable, or that it can't deal with serious social or personal issues. Indeed, genre fiction, because of its popularity, has a wider social reach than 'unrestricted' fiction. It is to say only that it has restrictions and it is the restrictions themselves that make readers read and enjoy it. Conversely, this division of 'open' and 'closed' fiction is not to praise all traditional literary fiction, examples of which can, of course, be dull, uninspiring, and cliché-ridden.

Genre, then, as a line of descent, is both crucial to the creation of literature and to reading and understanding books. But it is also, as 'genre fiction' or as branding for fiction books, delimiting, restricting: it threatens to limit what it is that literature can do. We might be both interested in and suspicious about genre.

Chapter 4
The past

Novels have always been interested in the past, in history and in memory. When the novel was still a relatively new art form at the beginning of the 19th century, it was profoundly shaped by the cultural and commercial success of Sir Walter Scott's historical fiction. Contemporary fiction is turning back to thinking about the past but often rejects the traditional historical novel by exploring memory, trauma, and the way the past haunts and possesses the present. Barack Obama famously cited one of William Faulkner's characters: 'The past is never dead. It's not even past.' Much contemporary fiction explores very different ways in which this is true. Of course, our relationship to the events of the past is always changing; as attitudes about the past change, historical research takes new directions and uses different resources and archives. Our stories about the past, formal and informal, private and public, shift and develop. Because we are, in part, shaped by the stories we tell about our pasts, these changes, in turn, mean that our sense of ourselves changes, too: our past is always about our present. Contemporary fiction not only reflects these quite normal changes but also investigates ways we relate not to just the events of the past but to our experience of 'pastness' itself.

The new historical novel

Interested in reading fiction about history? In reading about Boudicca or Ivan the Terrible or the Battle of Waterloo or Haitian struggles for independence? Turn to *What Historical Novel Do I Read Next?*, a huge reference work, detailing thousands of historical novels and novelists, broken down by period, event, and character. Suggesting that the 'historical novel' is a work set at least fifty years before it was written (Walter Scott suggested sixty years), it reveals that the 19th century is by far the most popular period for historical fiction (over twice the number of entries for the 17th century, its nearest rival) but that Elizabeth I is the most popular historical character, narrowly beating George Washington. Rather charmingly, it also rates novels under a subheading of 'historical accuracy': many are 'filled with authentic period details that convincingly capture the period', some are only 'convincing', and one entry, under this heading of 'historical accuracy', just reads 'missing' (I'll spare the book's blushes). Faced with *War and Peace*, this system of categorization collapses: it reads, simply and correctly, that it is 'one of the greatest novels ever written'.

This reference work neatly sums up the complex issues around traditional historical fiction: the fiction is caught between the need to be literary, invoking character, narrative, and so on, and the need to be historical, the need to be accurate to the record of the historical past and even, perhaps, didactic. More than this, its very location in the present raises the inescapable problem of anachronism, the way in which writing in the present unavoidably misrepresents the past. It can only write about the past using the concerns, preconceptions, ideas, thoughts, and language of the present. Historians, whose job it is to write about the past in the genre called 'history', usually deal with this problem simply by ignoring it. But when they do face it, they rightly point out that their form of historical writing refers to documents, archives, eye-witness accounts, the work of other historians, and so on, all expressed in footnotes and references for the reader to see and, if the reader is also keen or another historian, to check rigorously. Each proper work of history implicitly asks if, given the 'conventions' of the genre of history, its own account of the past is a fair one. But novels, which, as I have suggested earlier, can say anything, just don't have these conventions and so the problems of anachronism are much more acute. The problems could be divided up into what could be called 'surface' anachronism (clocks striking in ancient Rome, as in Shakespeare's play *Julius Caesar*, or soldiers with the wrong number of buttons on their tunic) and what might be called 'deep' anachronism: the representation of the behaviour and attitudes of people in the past as if they were from the present, simply 'dressed up' in the clothes from a wardrobe in the past. The former seems relatively trivial, the latter potentially quite dangerous.

Indeed, the Marxist Hungarian critic of the historical novel, György Lukács, inspired by Walter Scott, wrote strongly against historical novels that flagrantly displayed this kind of 'deep anachronism', which he described as 'mere costumery'. For Lukács, historical fiction communicated and educated. It demonstrated 'by artistic means that historical circumstances and characters existed in precisely such-and-such a way': it had to be profoundly rooted in historical moments. In this way, historical novels would show the 'derivation of the individuality of the characters from the historical peculiarity of their age', the way people are of their time (and not merely 'like us' dressed up with period props) and so, crucially for him, historical fiction would reveal what he took to be the very processes of history itself. It is no coincidence, for Lukács, that historical fiction was popular at times of great social change and unrest when, for a Marxist, the 'revolutionary laws' of 'history' itself were being made manifest. But even if writers could, by an astonishing act of imagination, write a genuinely 'historical' novel untouched by their own location in the present, Lukács's thought suggests that there is a 'necessary anachronism' in that characters have to 'to express feelings and thoughts about real, historical relations in a much clearer way than the actual men and women of the time could have done'. The crude, comedic way of expressing this idea would be to have a character step out of their house one May morning in 1601, breathe in deeply, and say,

'Well, here I am in Shakespeare's London, where genius fills the air.' But even more sophisticated writing, in the end, betrays this same sort of anachronism, this impossibility of representing the past without the present.

Much traditional historical fiction written today just ignores this problem of anachronism, happy with 'mere costumery', or, as Hilary Mantel's two Man Booker Prize winners *Wolf Hall* (2009) and *Bring Up the Bodies* (2012) do, gently covers up the issue by, for example, using 21st-century language naturalistically in the Tudor period. However, other contemporary fiction set in the past positively engages with exactly this and revels in the fact that our current ideas actively shape versions of the past: these might be called historical revisionist novels. They make explicit the problem of anachronism and admit that these stories seemingly about the past are inescapably about the present. Historical fiction acts as a mirror to our contemporary concerns, at its best in trying to rewrite the history that is 'taken for granted' in different ways. Perhaps the leading example of this historical revisionist novel in contemporary fiction is the huge interest in the Victorian period. Indeed, this interest in the Victorians—which is found in literary fiction, genre fiction (science fiction's 'steampunk', for example, and in detective fiction)—is so widespread that there is even a name for it: neo-Victorianism.

Jean Rhys's powerful novel *Wide Sargasso Sea* (1966) is perhaps one of the earliest and most influential of these neo-Victorian revisons. It retells the story of Charlotte Brontë's *Jane Eyre* (1847) from the point of view of the 'madwoman in the attic', the first Mrs Rochester. In doing so, it not only revealed Victorian racism, sexism, and unkindness but also modern versions of, and contemporary complicity with, precisely these. If the world of the 1960s thought it had escaped the oppressive, old-fashioned Victorians, this revision of a widely loved classic novel queried that idea of progress. John Fowles's early postmodern novel (it has three endings) *The French Lieutenant's Woman* (1969) is also part of the origin of neo-Victorianism. In it a hectoring authorial voice tells off various Victorians for their hypocrisy and moral failings, and, in one case, sends an admittedly unpleasant Victorian matron to hell. A. S. Byatt's love story *Possession: A Romance* (1990) won the Booker Prize (as it was then known) and it also retells or reshapes how we see both the Victorian protagonists and, at the same time, the contemporary academics studying the Victorian archive they have found. These historical novels stem in no small part, as Byatt writes, from 'the political desire to write the histories of the marginalized, the forgotten, the unrecorded'. That said, one of the most celebrated of these neo-Victorian revisionings has been the series of novels written by George MacDonald Fraser featuring Flashman, the bully from the popular Victorian novel by Thomas Hughes, *Tom Brown's School Days* (1857). In these meticulously researched historical novels, Flashman is a cowardly, sexist bully, generally unpleasant but superficially charming, who, in his sensational military adventures, always comes out on top like all great comedic villains in literature. In playing the same trick as Jean Rhys—reinhabiting a Victorian fiction—even these very different novels clearly point out the many hypocrisies of the Victorian period and our own. The Flashman novels highlight an obsession with celebrity and image, for example, and perhaps much more importantly—Fraser was a war veteran who saw action in Burma—question our faulty, glamorous vision of war and military heroism.

Sarah Waters is perhaps the most interesting contemporary writer who best embodies this neo-Victorianism. Waters is very aware of the differences between the present and the historical past: indeed, she says that it is 'precisely the difference of the past that makes it exciting for me. I think we always need to be reminded that the moment we live in is very temporary. Historical fiction at its best can remind us of that.' Her neo-Victorian novel *Fingersmith* (2002) begins in a theatre in which *Oliver Twist* is being performed. This sets the tone both for the theatricality of the novel, in which everyone is acting a role and no one is what they seem, and for the setting, the criminal underclass of what can only be called Dickens's London. Indeed Sue, the first narrator of the novel, lives on Lant Street, where the young Dickens lived, and where his character Little Dorrit gets married (there's also a really nice pub there too, now, called, in a Victorian vein, *The Gladstone*). The theatricality reminds the reader of the 'mere costumery' jibe against historical fiction, and seems to stress that historical fiction in this mode *can only be* 'costumery'.

The novel is the story of two women who become involved in a complex criminal scheme and is full of astounding and dizzying plot twists. Like most historical novels, it's long, full of period detail, and does a tour through the Victorian sensation fiction it imitates: Here's a thieves' den in the Borough backstreets! Here's a madhouse! There's a remote country estate! A secret marriage! A violent dénouement in which secrets are revealed! Characters that resemble those in other novels appear: the villain, Gentleman, is like Bill Sikes. The Uncle is a twisted Mr Causabon from *Middlemarch*. But unlike many more straightforward historical fictions, and suggested by the very conscious reuse of the conventions of sensation fiction, *Fingersmith* is a revision.

Sarah Waters wrote a PhD titled 'Wolfskins and Togas' on writers who turned to historical fiction in order to find ways to represent non-straight sexuality in more oppressive times. (The writer Naomi Mitchison, who began writing in the 1920s, when faced with censorship of her work, turned to writing historical fiction because 'overt sex' was 'apparently...all right when people wear wolfskins and togas'.) In *Fingersmith*, the two main characters, while deceiving each other, fall for each other and, very strikingly in a Victorian novel, make love. The event is described twice, from each of their viewpoints. Much of the novel is involved with what literary critics call 'queering' the text: the ways in which, through the lens of a non-straight sexuality, moments of plot or stock clichés can be reused or will reappear in strange and different ways. For example, as the critic Kaye Mitchell argues, a pornography collection, central to the plot, is reused as 'a history of female pleasure and desire rather than a means of the objectification, imprisonment and abuse of women'.

Fingersmith is not just revising the Victorian novel by drawing attention to same-sex love (and to other characteristics: there is, for example, a great deal of very profane swearing, absent from real Victorian writers, which jars very interestingly with one's expectations). Waters argues that lesbian historical fiction allows us to 'identify a lesbian tradition that has been both routinely overlooked by the historical record and calculatedly expunged from it'. The novel is attempting to reshape our relations to traditions in the past not only by representing lesbians but drawing attention to a tradition of lesbian fiction in the novels we have from the past. In showing how there is a tradition of lesbians and gay men in fiction, it is a historical novel about, as it were, historical novels, and so invites us to rethink literary history. The main protagonist, Sue, can't read. Her lover, Maud, at the end of the novel, begins to teach her. Similarly, perhaps, the novel is insisting that we have been unable to read, or perhaps are only just beginning to read, a tradition of gay and lesbian writing. More than this, the novel also draws attention to the subtle codes and different constructions through which sexuality has always been shaped and expressed. However, to focus just on the representation of sexuality is to do this wide-ranging novel an injustice as it contains much more. For example, *Fingersmith* is also clearly about the limitations of class mobility for Victorians, making absolutely explicit what is present but much less clear in Dickens and in other Victorian writers. The aspirations of the novel's characters to escape poverty, and the difficulty of this, are also something that reflects on our contemporary context.

Memory and trauma

If the historical novel is one way of relating to the past, retelling the past to cast light on both it and us, there are other modes in which the relationship between the past and the present are interrogated. The historical novel, even in such self-conscious form as Waters's, is writing in a tradition going back to at least Walter Scott. Being in a tradition, inhabiting a tradition, is one of the main ways of relating to the past. We enact and re-enact family traditions (cooking a traditional meal; supporting the same football team), ethical, cultural, and religious ones (giving birthday presents, celebrating Christmas or Eid), and national traditions (Remembrance Day or Martin Luther King Day). Our moral behaviour, too, used to be shaped by traditions of moral thought. They are 'our' traditions, and make the past 'our' past and make us who we are. Even in rejecting a tradition we remain hooked into it, as that thing that we purposely reject and avoid. In this way, traditions are the strongest form of 'collective memory'.

Just as our own individual memories are, in the poet Wallace Stevens's phrase, a 'necessary fiction' of ourselves, the measure of our own self's continuity through time, so 'collective memory' marks our being in and with society. Indeed, as the philosopher Maurice Halbwachs argued, because our own memories are acquired in society, on scales ranging from families to nations, it is these social frameworks for memory that provide not just the content of our memories but form the very context for memory itself. For Halbwachs, memory is first social before it is individual. This goes a long way in explaining why our shared, collective memories are so important. In contrast to the traditional view of history written by historians, which divides up times and societies by sometimes arbitrary markers and seems to claim a neutral 'view from nowhere' (the Nobel Laureate William Golding called this 'academic' or 'campus' history), collective memory deals with the 'living traditions' we inhabit and enact—from religious celebrations to national memorials to support of sports teams to idiosyncratic family habits—and is embedded in our daily lives. (Golding called it 'history felt in the blood and bones' and was suspicious of it.) These collective memories are what bind communities together or, equally, push them apart. Just as a collective memory might work as a unifying force, so it is also possible to 'activate' a memory and reshape or divide a wider community. There is a powerful 'memory politics' to the ways in which memory is shaped and used, and it is a significant force in the world today. Partly this is because ways of 'living in' a tradition, these forms of collective memory, have been interrupted by the modern world, by the very experience of modernity. Some of these changes seem very positive to me: the expansion of human rights, the emancipation of women. Some are almost beyond judgement: rapid social and technological change, mass movement of peoples and ideas. And some—genocide, war, and mass murder—are evil, yet still part of modernity, and leave trauma and suffering in their aftermath. These more cultural and personal traumas all rework traditions and memories. Our relationships with the past can be traumatic.

The word trauma, which means 'wound' in Greek, was used by Freud and others in a more metaphorical sense to mean a 'psychological wound' in order to try to explain the behaviour of people who had suffered a terrible event. People who are 'traumatized' in this sense carry a special sort of wound. The event or events that befell them are so powerful and painful as to be incomprehensible: that is, they cannot be 'comprehended' or grasped by the psyche, cannot, as it were, be put into the person's story of themselves. This means that the memory of the event remains to haunt and disturb the person, as the memory is either repressed and ignored (and so comes back in complex and unpredictable ways) or constantly relived inside the mind as 'flashbacks' of images or behaviours.

Writing about the impact of traumatic events brings literature right to the edge of fiction, in the way David Shields and others discuss. Much that is written about terrible things that happen would better be called 'testimony', the personal telling of real events. Testimony brings with it responsibilities and demands on both author and reader. But, as I have suggested, these categories are blurry: no novel is ever free from its own history and development; and by the same measure, no work of testimony is free from the concepts we associate with novels, the shape of a narrative, its closure, the movement of sympathy. The telling of testimony and the telling of history are both constructed in that they are retold, after the events, shaped by things that are not simply the events. Yet, in fiction, precisely because it is free to say anything, there is often an access to the manipulation of collective memory. And to return to the second level of metaphor, there are traumas in collective memory as well, communal events in a traumatic past that are hard to speak about or to focus on. Fiction can bring these out: indeed, perhaps it is in fiction most of all that these cultural traumas are most often, painfully but perhaps also usefully, investigated.

One very successful Spanish novel, *Soldiers of Salamis* (2001, trans. 2004) by Javier Cercas, focuses on precisely this relationship between personal memory and traumatized collective memory. At the beginning of the 21st century, Spanish writers and historians were beginning to challenge what was called the 'pact of silence', the tacit agreement that the horrors and atrocities of the Civil War should not be mentioned or discussed in public for the sake of Spain's democracy. The collective trauma was repressed. The protagonist of *Soldiers of Salamis* is, like the author, also called Javier Cercas: this is the first sign that this novel, like many that deal explicitly with memory, sets up a complex and new relation between memory, fiction, and the historical record. The fictional Cercas is mourning his father, his failed first marriage, and his stalled career as a writer, and during these griefs he becomes obsessed with the story of Rafael Sánchez Mazas. Mazas is a person from the historical record, a writer and a founder member of the Spanish Falange. What especially grabs the fictional Cercas's attention is Mazas's escape from a Republican firing squad in the last days of the war, and, in the subsequent search, his encounter with a Republican soldier who sees him but refuses to give him away: 'the solder stared at him for a few seconds and then, without taking his eyes off him, shouted "There's nobody over here," turned and walked away'. Mazas escapes into the forest, eventually finds shelter and is aided by three deserters. He returns to play a role in Franco's dictatorship and, as Cercas says, there's 'a street named after him in Bilbao'.

This merciful moment of 'not shooting' in Mazas's story obsesses the fictional Cercas and he tries to find the truth of it by researching records, finding survivors, and chasing leads while, at the same time, he is slowly (and implicitly) recovering from his own personal traumas. He replies to his newspaper editor who asks if he is writing a novel that 'I don't write novels any more...besides it's not a novel, it's a true story.' This story becomes an evolving metaphor for overcoming the 'pact of silence' and for the potential healing of Spain. Cercas contentiously tries to lay these horrors to rest in explicitly discussing the events from the experience of both sides. His new girlfriend is shocked by this, complaining that he is focusing on a fascist, not on a respectable leftist.

However, in the third part of the novel, Cercas traces a Republican solider called Miralles, who was present at the shooting from which Masas escaped: he may (or may not) be the man who let Masas go. Miralles is a scarred veteran who fought not only for the Republicans, but as a volunteer for the Free French in Africa and in Europe: he is the novel's Republican counterweight to Masas. The title of the novel comes from the thinker Oswald Spengler (1880–1936), whose book *The Decline of the West* (1918) helped shape the atmosphere of interwar Europe. Spengler claimed that small groups of soldiers have always saved the West, as a small group of soldiers did at the Battle of Salamis (480 BCE), saving the Greeks from the Persians. Miralles, it is clear, is precisely one of these small groups of soldiers, but he is far from the hero of some fascist mythology. He is a leftist, but not deeply political, rough, earthy, and he fought not against some version of foreign 'Persians' but against fascists in Spain and Europe. He has a brutal, unglamorous version of what heroism really is: not some act from a clichéd story, but a contingent chance of doing the right thing at the right moment.

Yet, and this is Cercas's 'memory politics', Miralles is seen to dance a profoundly felt *pasodoble*, both by a friend of Cercas (a fictionalized version of the Chilean novelist Roberto Bolaño) and, during the Civil War, by Masas himself during his imprisonment. This *pasodoble* becomes a symbol of a 'real' Spain, deeper than the one divided by the Nationalists and the Republicans. It is this idea that is the seed for a healing of the trauma in collective memory. Miralles tells Cercas of the names of his companions who died, heroes in his unglamorous sense, during the Civil War and the Second World War. These men, after whom no streets are named in Bilbao, are seen as just as much part of what Spain really and profoundly is, and are brought back into the span of collective memory. They are 're-membered' as the body of memory is healed together. Indeed, Cercas fantasizes about creating a new pseudo-family, adopting Miralles as a sort of replacement father, marrying his girlfriend, having children. At the end of the novel he is travelling home, content, the past at rest, and able to move 'onwards, onwards, ever onwards'. The story of both Masas and Miralles, their (possible) moment of merciful connection and trust in a 'deeper' Spain, changes the protagonist and helps him heal his personal and, it's implied, Spain's collective trauma. This resolution might look a little too straightforward. After all, the image of a 'deep Spain' summed up in a dance is itself a political image, claiming a 'real' Spain of those who share this feeling. Soldiers, even if earthy and not honoured in their own country, are still heroic and fit a version of the fascist myth of power and violence. But the novel is a genuine engagement with the problems of collective memory.

However, as I've suggested, collective memory is not simply shaped by the past, it's not just (as Golding says) 'felt in the blood and bones'. In a more rootless modern world, other, perhaps more questionable and manipulative, forces seek to exploit memories, wounds, and traumas rather than heal them. Aleksandar Hemon's *The Lazarus Project* (2008), an allusive, melancholic novel that is funny and awful at the same time, circles around exactly this and so is an example of another form of relationship to the past.

This novel tells two stories which cross over and interweave. The first draws on events from the historical record, the story of a young Jewish immigrant to the United States, Lazarus Averbuch, and the controversy over his death. On 2 March 1908, Averbuch visited the chief of police of Chicago, George Shippy, on some undefined errand. Shippy and his driver, taking him for an anarchist intent on murder, shot him dead. This killing is the focus for a panic, with more than a hint of anti-Semitism, stirred up by the yellow press and others, about anarchists and non-Americans threatening the state. Moving seamlessly between historical sources and fiction, the novel explores this panic, its manipulation by the press, and the impact of this on Averbuch's sister, Olga, who eventually returns to Europe. (Some critics have seen this as a response to hysteria over 9/11—the al-Qaeda terrorist attacks of 11 September 2001—in the United States.) The second strand concerns a struggling, underemployed Bosnian-American writer, Vladimir Brik, who is in an unhappy marriage. Brik, by chance, left Bosnia before the war there, and while shaped by the war (the country that was his home has changed utterly), feels keenly his lack of experience of that war. Receiving a grant, Brik uses it to trace Averbuch's story back to Europe and, at the same time, trace his own roots to Bosnia, accompanied by his friend, Rora, a photographer. Rora, who did live through the war in Bosnia, is an endless source of stories which may or may not be true, stories which both fascinate Brik and make him, in a way, envious of his friend's experience. These war stories, true or exaggerated like the press panic over Averbuch and anarchism, are almost where the past is turned from experience into collective memory, as if 'it may not have happened but it was like that'. During their journey, Brik thinks about his failing marriage, about his identity as a Bosnian-American, and about his own writing. Finally arriving back in Sarajevo, Brik feels 'like a ghost'. It is an 'uncanny' experience (following Freud, the word uncanny in German is *unheimlich*, un-home-ly), Brik is 'invisible...Nobody seemed to remember me. Home is where somebody notices your absence.' The stories he has told his wife about his home town no longer have any purchase, they have disappeared. His home has gone.

The novel is left unresolved. Averbuch and Olga's story is never finally explained nor their roots traced (although it seems likely that Olga died in the Holocaust) and the stories in the press remain unanswered. Brik's own life is left in flux, at the mercy of trying and failing to find meaning in his own personal experiences and, through the stories of his friends, his 'collective' experience as a Bosnian. While the novel is about 'living after' some appalling event, like Lazarus from the Christian Gospels, it is, in its title, a *project*, something thrown, *project*ed towards an end or goal, not a finished thing. The trauma here, unlike in *The Soldier of Salamis*, is not healed or resolved. Rather the novel is about exactly the swirl of memory and identity, and the nature and role of stories, about the ways in which memories are formed, about the different ways we relate to the traumatic past in stories. Brik writes that he had told his wife 'stories of my childhood and immigrant adventures' but had found himself:

> longing for the Sarajevo way of doing it – Sarajevans told stories ever aware that the listener's attention might flag, so they exaggerated and embellished and sometimes downright lied to keep it up. You listened, rapt, ready to laugh, indifferent to doubt or implausibility...Disbelief was permanently suspended, for nobody expected truth or information, just the pleasure of being in the story and, maybe, passing it off as their own. It was different in America: the incessant perpetration of collective fantasies makes people crave the truth and nothing but the truth—reality is the fastest American commodity.

The relation to the past as yet unfixed and unhealed is enacted in the telling of stories, not in the content of the stories themselves.

Haunting and possession

Brik and others often speak of finding themselves 'haunted' by the past. The philosopher Jacques Derrida offered another very potent metaphor for the relation between the past in the present which drew on this sort of idea. Because his philosophical approach (called 'deconstruction') questioned common-sense platitudes and ingrained philosophical habits of thought, but also right- and left-wing beliefs, he was pressed by intellectuals on the left in the 1970s and 1980s to clarify his views on his relationship to Marx (intellectuals are quite as worried as everyone else by the question of inhabiting a tradition). In the early 1990s, he answered these demands in his book *Spectres of Marx*, which reflects on *Hamlet* and begins with Marx's famous warning from the beginning of the *Communist Manifesto* (a 'spectre is haunting Europe: the spectre of communism'). The past, he suggested, is like a ghost: it haunts us. Just as Hamlet's father's ghost comes to Hamlet and demands he take action to revenge his murder, so the ghost of the traditions of the past (in this specific case, the intellectual and political tradition of Marxism, but his point is much wider) comes to us and speaks in the present. In the past that haunts us, it is as if we hear the voices of ghosts, the voices of the dead. Ghosts—in *Hamlet* and in most fiction—are very peculiar: they are both there, in front of you, clanking their chains, and yet not there, insubstantial nothings. They are both alive and dead, active spirits of dead people, present and absent *at the same time*. This makes them both hard and interesting to think about, and, of course, very unsettling: it's just not clear in which categories they belong.

But this powerful metaphor for how the past relates to us, as 'haunting', is not altogether right. In modernity, we can, certainly, go actively to seek the past, creating and choosing to inhabit our own traditions (although one might ask: is there a difference somewhere between a tradition that you 'just do', as it were, unthinkingly, and one that you consciously and thoughtfully choose to take up?). We can, to use Derrida's metaphor, speak to the ghost, engage with a tradition. But equally, we can simply ignore the ghost: in fact, Hamlet considers this option himself. A less dramatic example of the limits of haunting is our relationship to statues. Cities worldwide and especially the older European former imperial cities are full of statues. These statues are, in a sense, dead people: ghosts which address us. However, how often do we pay attention to these ghosts and how often, in fact, do we simply pass by them and not even see them? Our relationship to haunting is like that. We don't need to be haunted, we can simply ignore the ghosts, ignore the past conceived in that way.

So although I don't think 'haunting' is quite the right word, there is something powerful in this idea which is picked up by contemporary fiction. If we don't inhabit the past, the past certainly inhabits us. We live in it, in the buildings we use; we tell it, in the stories we tell; and, of course, we speak it in the languages we speak. Our language we inherit from the past, and, although we change it, we change it slowly over time with implicit rules we inherit from the past. In fact, to swop one sort of Halloween vocabulary of horror word for another, more acute one, the past does not haunt us but *possesses* us. This possession is not a whole, in the way that traditions used to be, perhaps, but rather seizes us in fragmented and uncanny ways.

This idea is at the centre of Nicola Barker's huge novel *Darkmans* (2007). Rather like the title of *Fingersmith*—old slang for a thief or (appropriately, given the novel) a midwife—'darkmans' is an old thieves' cant word for night. Set in the middle of the first decade of the 21st century, in Ashford, Kent in the UK, where the forces of the new (the rebuilding for the Channel tunnel, motorways, new roads, and roundabouts) run up directly against the old (an ancient medieval town, the landscape, and the coast), *Darkmans* tells the story of several linked characters and of possession.

The characters are possessed by obsessions, by revenge, by grief, and, in a literalizing metaphor that takes over the book, by the past in the form of a mischievous-to-the-point-of-evil jester from the late medieval period.

Daniel Beede, a former merchant seaman, is obsessed with the past, specifically a mill which has been taken down and reassembled: however, the tiles from this mill were stolen by a developer and Beede is, it seems, possessed by trying to enact a slow vengeance on him. He is, it seems, paying an art forger a huge amount of money to forge perfectly normal things in the developer's home (a mug, for example) with tiny unsettling things wrong with them, to create a sense of unease and un-at-homeliness. Kane is Beede's estranged son. He illegally deals prescription painkillers because he is psychically paralysed by witnessing the abortive assisted suicide and lingering, painful death of his mother. Gaffar, a Kurd and former small-time gangster, is employed by Kane to run errands. They also know Elen, a chiropodist, who has a birthmark and may (or may not) be a witch, her husband Dory/Isadore, who is pretending to be German, and their strangely precious and fey child Fleet. Dory has episodes where he loses his memory and behaves in a strange way (abandoning his car and stealing a horse, for example). At first these are thought of as madness, but slowly it becomes clear it may be that the spirit of a jester called John Scogin has possessed him. He behaves in unsettling ways, hurts his wife: the son, Fleet, may in fact be Scogin's son. A story that recurs in the novel tells how Scogin imprisoned several beggars in a barn, and then burnt the barn down—his appearance in the novel is often accompanied by the smell of woodsmoke, and the novel is obsessed by fire and images of fire. The stories about this court jester appear in fragments of historical research throughout the novel and, indeed, he was a historical person. Barker, on the Man Booker Prize website, says:

> As soon as I found out about him I was completely bewitched. He was such an important historical figure at the time—one of the

first books ever printed in the English language was a book of his jokes. He was enormously famous and influential in the courts of both Edward IV and Richard III. He was one of the first educated jesters. Before Scogin jesters were generally just fools. Scogin merely pretended to be one. He struck me as being a very modern creature. He was cruel, ruthless and a terrifying opportunist. Sometimes I felt almost anxious about reaching out, blindly, into the darkness and drawing him into my narrative—he scares me—but I felt that he generated a special kind of energy in the text that only a real person could.

Scogin also seems to inhabit, from time to time, other characters: Kane, for example, and Beede, in one rather horrifying scene that occurs in a disorienting gap in the novel (all we're given is the set-up and the horrible aftermath). But this sense of possession runs right through the novel. Kane's favourite novel is Philip K. Dicks's *Beyond Lies the Wub*, which concerns the possession of human space explorers by an alien ('the Wub'). Fleet, possessed perhaps by Scogin, is obsessed by making a huge matchstick model of the cathedral at Albi, a building half cathedral and half fortress haunted by the brutal suppression of the Albigensian heresy.

But the central form of possession in the novel is language itself. The novel is reminding us that, spookily, it isn't us who use language but rather, language that uses us. The text is possessed by etymology. Characters say things like 'Liber is Latin for free. It's at the root of the modern English words liberty and libertine': our everyday language is possessed by the past. Characters' language becomes unstable in time: Fleet asks a fisherman if he can look 'at your mathek, please?' and, until it is realized that 'mathek' is an old word for maggots, his meaning is unclear. More, in a recurring trope, characters fumble chronologically through the whole history of a language to get to what they have to say. To say water one stutters 'Weit...vaat...vaad...votur...vater...water'; stunned by blood, another goes 'Reudh...Ruber...Rood...Rud...Red...Red... Blut-red'; Kane asks for his 'Bat ... beit ... bait ... boat'; and Dory, while possessed by John, considers his wife's mole 'mal...mole... moll...moll...molest...moelstus' (he goes on, darkly sinister, 'surely there must be some kind of *joke* in this?'). In these whole histories of words, associations swim to the surface and are made clear, as are their continual, if subliminal, impact on us. The words we use shape how we think and find ourselves in the world: whereas we can choose to ignore statues and ghosts (they are 'outside' us) we can't ignore the very words we use precisely because they shape us. The novel also uses an unusual form of free indirect speech, tiny little inserted italicized comments that interrupt and punctuate the main narrative, acting as often humorous asides or comments on the main part of the novel. While it's sometimes clear which character these are supposed to be 'from' it becomes increasingly hard to tell 'who' is speaking, until slowly it begins to feel as if the book itself is commenting on its own text.

Just as the people who are possessed lose their memory, so, as John's mischief increases throughout the novel, the novel too becomes increasingly disjointed and it is hard to tell what is going on. Gaps and strange shifts create a sort of narrative nausea. Dory may have set fire to a row of houses; Beede's revenge may be totally unnoticed; Kane and Beede may have begun some form of reconciliation; Elen may be having an affair. The book is also full of tiny odd errors: Kane is much too young to have sat 'O-level' exams (these exams, sat by English children at sixteen, were replaced by GCSEs in 1988) yet refers to doing so; he is also familiar with pop music that is not from his period (which isn't a mistake, *per se*, but, as it were, rings oddly in the ear); people suddenly find themselves not quite where they should be; crucial if tiny moments of narrative are occluded and missed out. But then, at the end of the novel, the forger, a woman called Peta Borough, explains that Beede had hired her to put a tiny 'fault into each piece...to help generate this indefinable sense of unease', which is what the novel does too, drawing attention to its own sense of being a novel, to its possession.

Indeed, the sense that it is a mystery or a sort of a ghost story, and that this deserves a dénouement or revelation of some sort is central and possesses the reader. And yet, this possession is fragmented and broken because no real dénouement or closure occurs: it is in this sense a 'shaggy ghost story'.

This theme of *possession* by the past is not unique to Barker. It underlies many genre fictions: the idea of the secret from the past that leaks out, in a thriller, or the idea that the past compels action. *Darkmans* is neither a critique of the present (in the way that the sexual politics of Waters's work might be seen to be) nor a praising of the past. Rather, both the present and the past are revealed to be pretty horrid: many characters allude to the similarities, links, between the medieval and the modern. In this, as in other innovations in form, *Darkmans* reflects the work of a previous generation of novelists: from Martin Amis, Waters inherits the drug-dealing slick modernity of Kane; from Angela Carter, the literary and philosophical possibilities of magic and 'unreal' events (the possession); from W. G. Sebald she takes not only a sense of the odd bleakness and yet plenitude of the past of the English landscape but also, more strongly, the unavoidable sense of the connection of all sorts of seemingly disparate things together and, perhaps, the melancholy this engenders. And from Thomas Pynchon, the great American postmodern novelist, she inherits not only the length and encyclopedic nature of the novel and the uncertainties and paranoia of modern living, but also the sense that to engage with modern life, it must engage with motion and complexity. However, if in Pynchon's American cities this involves only an oneiric sense of newness and lack of permanence, in England the same sort of relation is evoked by the feeling not of a haunting by the past but of a possession that is complex and sinister. Barker's novel works out a contemporary relationship to the past, one not of inhabiting a tradition or being haunted but one in which we are possessed by aspects of the past, by and through our language, and one from which we cannot escape. One in which we don't even realize that we need to escape, in which the idea of escape cannot even occur.

Conclusion

In this chapter, I've tried to explore emblematic versions of the new ways in which contemporary fiction engages with the past. Sarah Waters's *Fingersmith* clearly and cunningly admits its 'costumery', and so directly challenges the more established conventions of the historical novel by making explicit the anachronism implicit in all historical fiction. Yet at the same time it deploys this self-consciousness to make a point about the ways in which lesbians have been written out of history and fiction, while providing a thrilling plot. Javier Cercas's *Soldiers of Salamis* engages in the memory politics of Spanish history in an attempt to heal the collective trauma of the Civil War, while Aleksandar Hemon's *The Lazarus Project* finds itself exploring not the resolution of collective trauma but precisely the confused and complex moments in which events are turned into conflicting and contested memories. History haunts Hemon, and others, but a ghost can be ignored. In contrast, Nicola Barker's long and experimental novel *Darkmans* tries to focus precisely on what I have called 'possession': the ways in which, unavoidably or unknowingly, the past holds and shapes people in the present.

Of course, these don't represent all the possible ways to engage with the past: for example, Anne Michaels, in *Fugitive Pieces* (1997), her beautiful and lyrical novel about the memory of the Holocaust, writes that the past is like the layers of rock on which we stand, perhaps unknown to us but still there, and it rises within us in strange ways. Péter Nádas's *Parallel Stories* (2005, trans. 2012) is an encyclopedic epic, covering the whole history of Middle Europe, centring on Hungary, from the Second World War; Patrik Ouředník's *Europeana* (2001 trans. 2005) retells a similar history laconically, laced with black humour.

Some critics suggest that there has been a turn to the past in contemporary fiction because novelists are finding the new technologies too hard to write about, or because the past is somehow easier than the present as a subject, or out of a new conservatism in writing. As I've suggested, because of the nature of anachronism, this is a strange idea: whatever the problems of the present, writing about the past *is* writing about the present, whether the fiction evades this fact or, more interestingly, faces it head on.

I think what is more interesting is both *why* and *how* the past has become a subject for contemporary writing in these new and challenging ways. The great philosopher of history, Hayden White, pointed out nearly fifty years ago that the 'modern artist does not think very much of what used to be called the "historical imagination"' and indeed that 'one of the distinctive characteristics of contemporary literature is its underlying conviction that the historical consciousness must be obliterated if the writer is to examine with proper seriousness those strata of human experience which it is modern art's peculiar purpose to disclose'. He adds that many, many great writers reflected 'the conviction voiced by Joyce's Stephen Dedalus, that history is the "nightmare" from which Western man must awaken if humanity is to be served and saved': the past cannot save us or help us and is not the subject for serious literature. This attitude correlates, too, with the disappearance of Scott and the work of other historical novelists from the 'canon' as well as with the wide-ranging sense that 'historical fiction' is a second-rate, 'popular' form, using the past simply as an exotic background. At the time it was written, White's argument also reflected a dryness in the writing of what Golding called 'academic' history.

However, the world changes and continues to change. And with those changes, the pressure of the past on the present has become not less but more intense, more demanding. New national, cultural, personal stories about the past demand to be told and the traumas of history, often ignored (like the Spanish 'pact of silence') or passed over (like many colonial atrocities), seem to emerge anew and unhealed. In the West and in the formerly communist East, the end of the Cold War has led to profound re-evaluations of the past. The rise of globalization and the end of the postcolonial period, too, have reshaped everyone's past. More than this, the past itself, not just the histories told about the past, means something different from what it did. Historians have responded to this by writing new histories and sometimes new forms of history. Novelists, it seems to me, have been slower to do this. In the second half of the 20th century, while there were works of historical fiction which addressed almost any topic (*What Historical Novel Do I Read Next?*) these were of the same realist form as the traditional works of history. The novels in this chapter, and the many others of which they are only emblematic, are beginning to find innovative forms to represent the demands of our changing relationships to the past.

Chapter 5
The present

What radical evil really is I don't know, but it seems to me it
somehow has to do with the following phenomenon: making
human beings as human beings superfluous (not using them as
a means to an end, which leaves their essence as humans
untouched and impinges only on their human dignity; rather,
making them superfluous as human beings). This happens as
soon as all unpredictability—which, in human beings, is the
equivalent of spontaneity—is eliminated.

Hannah Arendt

The previous chapter addressed how contemporary fiction has
begun to find new ways of engaging with the past and so
reshaping the present. This chapter turns to the more
contentious issue of how contemporary fiction deals with
the—our—present.

But should literature deal with the present, as if it were a news
programme or had to have an agenda like a politician? As I've
suggested, because a novel can say anything, it might choose to
focus on something in the present or it might not: there can't be
programmatic rules about what a novel *has* to be about. However,
because, like us, fiction is bound into its time, it will inescapably
be in some way about the time of its writing, whether it explicitly
addresses the 'issues of the day' or not. (Perhaps the more a novel

tries to avoid these issues, the more it becomes implicitly about them.) But, then, what are the issues of the present? This is, in part, an absurd question. 'Everyone knows' what these are: globalization, economic disaster, race and gender inequality, the rapid changes in technology, the exploitation and movement of people around the world, terror and 'endless war', the degradation of the environment, and with all these, our changes in our conceptions of what it means to be human living today. Is there any common thread among these?

The great German Jewish thinker Hannah Arendt suggested that there is. She analysed the totalitarian regimes of the 20th century and argued that their core evil was the way in which they made human beings, as human beings, superfluous. First, these regimes removed individuals' rights as citizens (removed their human rights, we'd say today, as in no small part, human rights as a concept has been popularized precisely because of these totalitarian regimes). Second, by creating dire circumstances such as ghettos, death camps, or prison gulags, they set people against each other in struggling to survive, leading to 'the murder of the moral person in man'. Finally, they destroyed each person's individuality and potential for what Arendt called 'spontaneity, man's power to begin something anew out of his own resources'. Describing this process in an analogous way, the contemporary Italian philosopher Giorgio Agamben explores an ancient Greek distinction between *zoë*, which means 'life', the very quality of living that humans, animals, and all plants share, and *bios*, life as living in a world where we are recognized as individuals with rights, duties, relationships, nationalities, and so on, a world where we have an identity in addition to just life. *Bios* might even be extended to animals and even ecosystems, which are given meaning and shape—made into a world—by human interaction with them. The totalitarian regimes of the 20th century stripped *bios* from *zoë* from their (often imagined) enemies, leaving only what Agamben calls 'bare life'. And bare life is all too easily simply exterminated. While there are still totalitarian regimes today, they do not dominate the world, but, Arendt speculates:

> [we] may say radical evil has emerged in connection with a system in which all men have become equally superfluous... The danger of the corpse factories and holes of oblivion is that today, with populations and homelessness everywhere on the increase, masses of people are continuously rendered superfluous if we continue to think of our world in utilitarian terms. Political, social and economic events everywhere are in a silent conspiracy with totalitarian instruments devised for making men superfluous... Totalitarian solutions may well survive the fall of totalitarian regimes.

The stripping of *bios* from *zoë*, this totalitarian solution, still seems to emerge in different forms in the contemporary world (in the total exploitation of migrant workers, for example, or in responses to terrorism). What has this threat, or this truth, to do with the contemporary novel?

In the 19th century, some novels tried to sum up the 'state of the nation' (as novels by Dickens did) or to describe a nation's soul or identity (this is what Tolstoy attempted). And in the 20th century, some novelists tried to create meaning in what they saw as an absurd and meaningless universe: Joyce brought together, as one person, Odysseus, an epic hero, and Leopold Bloom, a mild advertising canvasser from Dublin in 1904. But in an age in which the risk is the simple disposableness of human beings as human beings, these larger tasks may be too much to accomplish. Instead, the novel—the very possibility of the novel, a form which can say anything—is perhaps one of very, very few indispensable markers of what it is just to be alive and human today. Just by telling its story, making something intelligible against this backdrop of human redundancy, a novel is a tiny but concrete resistance to the global and profound trends that threaten to make humans superfluous. More than this, through what Arendt called 'unpredictability' or 'spontaneity', through being new in form and content, they cannot only respond to the world around us but also be markers of hope for something better to come. This process of making things intelligible and the characteristic of spontaneity come together in the special form of *attention* that a novel can create.

A realization of this small but concrete sense is connected with what might be called a 'new humility' in the contemporary novel. In the past, novels were often credited with making significant political interventions: in the United States, for example, John Steinbeck's *The Grapes of Wrath* (1939) is said to have changed ideas about poverty as Harriet Beecher Stowe's *Uncle Tom's Cabin* (1852) challenged ideas about slavery. (Whether this was ever quite so clearly the case is not certain.) But a recurring theme in contemporary fiction is that the novel can no longer—if it ever could—compete with politics on political terms. The novel form looks pretty weak in comparison to the whole weight of power, suffering, exploitation, and destruction in the world, all the forces that, as Arendt says, make human beings superfluous. But that very realization, perhaps, is something recent novels, and perhaps contemporary writing as a whole, is coming to understand.

One example of what this special form of attention can achieve is in the later work of David Eggers. In 2006, he and Valentino Achak Deng published *What Is the What: The Autobiography of Valentino Achak Deng*. Even the title asks questions (how can Eggers write someone else's autobiography?). It is the riveting true story of Deng's life in Sudan, his escapes from various atrocities perpetrated upon him and his people, his life in a refugee camp, and his subsequent life in America. It includes citations from historical documents and a lecture on the colonial history of Sudan. But it's told in two books. The first book is a long flashback, set while Achak is being robbed in his Atlanta apartment. The second takes place during the next day and includes his visit to hospital and return to one of his jobs.

Not only does this (very unsettling) frame destroy, from the beginning, any sense of narrative redemption but it makes clear that the United States is far from the answer to the problems faced by Achak and other Sudanese refugees and exiles. Achak writes that 'when I first came to this country, I would tell silent stories...to people who wronged me...I would glare at them, staring, silently hissing a story to them. *You do not understand*, I would tell them. *You would not add to my suffering if you knew what I have seen.*' Indeed, throughout, he addresses people silently in order to tell them his story: a child belonging to the robbers who tie him up, a receptionist at the hospital, the members of the health club at which he works are all silently told part of his story, and addressed like this. They seem unwilling to grasp the events whereas in contrast the widespread community of the Sudanese diaspora—in contact by mobile phone and Internet—are seen as comprehending and supporting. This is a morally serious and politically engaged book which draws attention to the plight of the Sudanese.

Eggers, who with Nínive Clements Calegari co-founded 826 Valencia, a charitable institution that teaches children to read and has now spread across the United States, also set up a foundation with Valentino Achak Deng. This organization aims 'to increase access to education in post-conflict South Sudan by building schools, libraries, teacher-training institutes, and community centres'. This is a serious action in the sphere of politics, of course. However, art cannot compete with politics in the terms set by politics: it needs to develop and respond in its own terms. *What Is the What* does this in the ways in which it draws attention to the world.

Another contemporary example is Junot Diaz's *The Brief Wondrous Life of Oscar Wao* (2007). The epigram to the novel comes from a comic, the *Fantastic Four*, and is said by a cosmic villain who consumes whole planets for sustenance: 'of what import are brief, nameless lives...to Galactus?'

Indeed, to a planet-eating monster, or to the huge forces of globalization or terror or totalitarian regimes, each of us in all our uniqueness does seem utterly superfluous. And yet, the carefully cited word 'nameless' reminds me, at any rate, of both Wordsworth's poem 'Lines written a few miles above Tintern Abbey', in which he praises 'that best portion of a good man's life | His little, nameless, unremembered, acts | Of kindness and of love' and, more importantly here, the way that this idea is central to George Eliot's fiction. Inspired by Wordsworth's idea, she writes at the end of *Middlemarch* (her novel in part about the web of huge impersonal forces), that the 'growing good of the world is partly dependent on unhistoric acts; and that things are not so ill with you and me as they might have been, is half owing to the number who lived faithfully a hidden life, and rest in unvisited tombs'. To the protagonist of *The Brief Wondrous Life of Oscar Wao*, Oscar de Leon, a young Dominican-American, this is prophetic. It is, of course, in the name of 'nameless lives' that Galactus is regularly defeated by superheroes.

The Brief Wondrous Life of Oscar Wao is the story of a group of Dominican migrants to the United States, centrally Oscar, but also his parents and the overall narrator, Yunior. It's told in a mixture of languages, with footnotes, jumps in time, play and humour, multiple characters and perspectives: many of the tricks of postmodern writing. Yet it maintains a strong narrative and embraces a sense of closure—as I described in Chapter 2, it's the sort of contemporary novel that is 'after' postmodernism, not rejecting but developing beyond postmodern styles. It's also a strongly political and moral book, centrally because the story concerns what the narrator calls 'Fukú', the 'Curse and the Doom of the New World', brought by 'screams of the enslaved' from Africa. But the 'fukú ain't just ancient history, a ghost story from the past with no power to scare. In my parent's day, the fukú was real as shit, something your everyday person could believe in' because the curse was made real in the dictatorship of the Dominican republic by Rafael Trujillo, who died in 1961: if 'you even thought a bad thing about Trujillo, *fuá*, a hurricane would sweep your family out to sea, *fuá*, a boulder would fall out of a clear sky and squash you'. The novel is about the impact of living under terror which is passed down through generations, and about the insignificance of life in a dictatorship. That Diaz's epigram comes from a comic is important. The novel is saturated with pop culture and 'cult' references: Tolkien, *Star Wars*, pop music, the fantasy role-playing game *Dungeons and Dragons*, science fiction films and comics. Apart from showing how the novel is of the present, a life constructed by the popular texts and ideas that come to hand by chance, these things that are supposed to be superfluous to serious thought and action become, here, a source of meaning and resistance. One of the reasons the protagonist is so obsessed with fantasy, comics, and science fiction is precisely because these give a frame to both understanding the evils of dictatorship (Trujillo was 'our Sauron, our Arawn, our Darkseid, our Once and Future Dictator') and a counter to the sense of superfluousness this creates: the all-powerful Dark Lord is always overthrown by a small band of unlikely heroes. Yet, in this non-fantasy novel, this is not the case: it is about Oscar's 'brief' and in many ways superfluous life. What remains is not Oscar's resistance. What remains is the novel itself, its telling, its pretty joyous telling, and this is its stand against being made nothing.

The globalized novel

Both these novels are also about globalization. One is written by a Dominican-American and is about Dominica and its history; one is about America and Sudan: both are about the interaction of different national and personal histories. On the one hand, the impact of globalization can be seen to be positive on contemporary literature. From the beginning of the 20th century, literature and its study used to be neatly divided up into national categories—English, American, Spanish, and so on—and these national traditions were part of the 'national imagination', our sense of ourselves as English, American, Spanish. There were difficult cases, of course (Henry James was an American living in England; James Joyce an Irish writer living in exile in Europe: the work of both was 'adopted' as English). There were international influences, too. Some 1960s American novelists—Saul Bellow, Norman Mailer—were a huge influence on British novelists of the 1970s, for example. But in the main, these national categories remained fairly fixed. However, in the 1960s and 1970s, new novels and novelists from Africa, South America, and Asia began to become known all over the world. Their work was called, for example, 'African' writing (as if Chinua Achebe, a Nigerian novelist, spoke for a whole continent) or, in the UK context, 'Commonwealth writing'. By the 1980s, the name for non-Western writing was 'Postcolonial literature', as the assumption was made that it would all deal, to some degree, with the impact of Empire. The critic Fredric Jameson once argued that all postcolonial fictions were 'national allegories' because 'the story of the private individual destiny is always an allegory of the embattled situation of the public third world culture and society'. Yet even this name, and this idea of 'national allegory', betrayed a sort of a European and American 'post-imperial' idea about the rest of the world. After all, first, a novel can address anything, and, second, surely Empire and its disappearance, or its emergence in new forms, affect *both* the colonizer and the colonized. If a contemporary novel about getting married today in Mumbai is 'postcolonial', so, surely, is a contemporary novel about getting married today in Manchester. As the processes of globalization increased and changed in the 21st century, so the novel and the 'national imagination' have changed to reflect this. Writers not only move globally themselves, publish internationally, and so on, but it is impossible to limit their work to a 'national tradition' or their audience to one country. Even more work is read in translation (although many more novels are translated from English than into English). This positive view of globalization suggests that we are all becoming more cosmopolitan, more aware of different traditions from across the world, and perhaps more tolerant and socially aware ('Act locally, think globally').

On the other hand, a negative view suggests that globalization is simply the exploitation of the globally poor by the globally rich and the reduction of local traditions into fodder for a world market in culture and goods, another way of making people superfluous. Aravind Adiga's *The White Tiger* (2008) is an example of precisely this tension. Told in letters addressed to Wen Jiabao, the then Premier of China, but also told with diurnal interruptions that echo *1001 Nights*, the novel is the story of Balram Halwai and his slow, and partially criminal, rise in business. In the novel, it is precisely the impact of globalization—especially in Delhi—that allows the protagonist to move from his caste-bound life in rural India to greater freedom and success, and so to challenge an older, oppressive form of life. Yet the cost of this is the loss of some part of his integrity and the damage he does to others. More than this, paradoxically, the novel is told in free and flowing English which the protagonist admits is, in fact, beyond him: in representing someone from rural India, Adiga seems to admit that he could not use the language of rural India. This is not to criticize the author, but to draw attention to the tensions of globalization at the level of plot and at the level of form. The risk of globalization is that it makes people feel not connected to each other in a cosmopolitan world, but, instead, feel redundant as human beings in the face of huge impersonal global forces. But there are more even more acute forms of this.

Literature in the face of 'endless war'

For most of the second half of the 20th century, the threat of total nuclear annihilation hung heavily over the world and, of course, this threat still exists. But now, of all the forces which threaten to make people superfluous in the world, the one that has received the most attention in the fiction of the last ten years is international terrorism and the sense of 'endless war'. Terrorism is not new, of course, but globalization has changed it. Indeed, the scale, shock, and surprise of the mass murder of 9/11, of other terrorist events, and of the 'endless war' that seems to flow from them is still being assimilated into the cultural life of the world. In responding to terror in the present, to the way that it makes people disposable, different novels have adopted different strategies.

Despite its shocking nature, 9/11 did not really come out of the blue: tensions in the interconnected globe had been increasing for years. Salman Rushdie, in *Fury* (published in the United States on 4 September 2001), wrote that the 'whole world was burning on a shorter fuse... Human life was now lived in the moment before the fury, when the anger grew, or the moment during—the fury's hour, the time of the beast set free—or in the ruined aftermath of a great violence, when the fury ebbed and chaos abated... craters—in cities, in deserts, in nations, in the heart—had become commonplace.' Rushdie himself had become the focus of some of these tensions when he was the victim of a fatwa calling for his death, issued in 1989 by the Ayatollah Khomeni, the religious leader of revolutionary Iran. Khomeni ruled that Rushdie's novel *The Satanic Verses* was blasphemous. Kenan Malik, in his study *From Fatwa to Jihad*, argues that while this was more a response to 'inter-Islamic strife both inside and outside Iran' it 'gave notice of a new Islam'. One of Salman Rushdie's great themes as a writer is the relationship of East and West: his novels both portray and exemplify the benefits of international and intercultural exchange and, at the same time, point out the violence, exploitation, greed, evil, and human frailty in this same exchange. One of his more pessimistic novels, *Shalimar the Clown* (2005), centres on terror and terrorism. Through it, like a chorus, a sense of disaster echoes: 'the time of demons had begun'; the 'age of reason was over, he was telling her, as was the age of love. The irrational was coming into its own. Strategies of survival might be required'; an 'age of fury was dawning and only the enraged could shape it'. Like all Rushdie's novels, there are many strands of narrative that weave over each other, here embodied in the four central characters. Shalimar, an actor and a clown, and Boonyi, a dancer, grow up, fall in love, and wed in their village of Pachigam in Kashmir, presented as a tolerant paradise in which Hindus and Muslims live and work together. However, following the Partition of India and Pakistan, this tolerant and friendly village is destroyed and disaster comes. Max Ophuls, a Jewish resistance hero and intellectual originally from Alsace—like Kashmir, a disputed territory—is posted as the US ambassador to India. He sees Boonyi dance and is entranced, while she sees in him an escape to a more exciting life. She becomes his mistress and Shalimar is left, bitter and trapped by an oath he had made to her: 'Don't you leave me now, or I'll never forgive you, and I'll have my revenge, I'll kill you and if you have any children by another man, I'll kill the children also.' Boonyi does have a child with Max, India, who is spirited away and brought up in the West by Max and his wife, and it is with India—fierce, independent, confused—that the novel begins and ends. Even in this brief summary, much that is typical of Rushdie emerges: the relationship between the personal and the political (Max and Boonyi are not only characters in their own right but allegorical characters for the United States and India); the sheer complexity of the relationships between 'East' and 'West'; betrayal, in history (the end of the tolerant Kashmir) and in love, both with a sense of inevitable violence and tragedy.

Shalimar leaves Kashmir, as it is destroyed by war and terrorism, and ascends into the mountains to Forward Camp 22, a terrorist training centre. Here he meets an 'Iron Mullah' who preaches an Islamist fundamentalism: 'It is not possible to shoot straight,' he says 'if the way you see things is all screwed up.' Yet Shalimar is not really concerned with ideology and violent Jihad, but with his own mission of revenge. Crucially, I think, for the meaning of the novel, this mismatch is true of everyone in the camps. Others hear him talking in his sleep about Boonyi and his revenge but 'nobody cared ... because all the other fighters were murmuring too...The murderous rage of Shalimar the clown...was just one of many stories, one small particular untold tale in a crowd of such tales, one miniscule portion of the unwritten history of Kashmir.' However, he pretends to be 'converted' in a performance of such acting skill he convinces the mullah and almost himself. Once trained, he kills for various terrorist groups, but is all the time working towards his own personal revenge. It seems to me that this strategy of engagement with terrorism is somehow flawed. In the world, of course no one has unmixed motives, but the novel is saying more than this. The personal revenge plot means that the wider political concerns which the novel invoked actually disappear. It is rather as if in setting out to be about terrorism, even partly allegorically, the novel can't fully face this and has to turn away. One symptom of this emerges as the novel finishes without ending, with Shalimar and his daughter (who has trained herself to be nearly as skilled a killer as her father) launching into an attack on each other: and the novel stops just at that moment, frozen. It might also mean that the novel as a form simply can't engage with politics in this way.

If *Shalimar the Clown* took as a protagonist a sort of terrorist assassin, Jonathan Safran Foer's second novel, *Extremely Loud and Incredibly Close* (2005), utilizes a different strategy to come to terms with the experience of terror by focusing on a victim, or, even more poignantly, the child son of a victim of terrorism. Oskar Schell is a precocious (but not obnoxious) nine-year-old boy, who has lost his father in the World Trade Center attacks. The novel tells the story of his mourning and his attempt to come to terms with the loss. He decides that his father has left a secret for him and makes his way around New York trying to find the lock that fits a key he had discovered in his father's bedroom just after 9/11. There's no question that the story is moving. The novel doesn't miss a trick to make you feel sorry for this clever and very sad little nine-year-old (and indeed, any novelist who couldn't make a reader feel sorry for a boy in this position probably shouldn't be a novelist). But this means, really, that the book is *too* moving

71

and the self-conscious childishness means that the novel is overly sentimental. But this isn't simply an aesthetic flaw: the sentimentality and choice of a child narrator go to the core of the novel. They give the novel licence to portray the events of 9/11 with a childlike simplicity. For example, there is an uncomplicated declaration that the leader of the cadre of terrorists, Mohammed Atta, 'was evil'. This may be, but no real person is so uncomplicated or so simply a fairy-tale monster, and to make them so, through the choice of a child narrator, is to oversimplify. Oskar has an extended daydream where he reimagines the planes hitting the towers:

> I imagined the last second, when I would see the pilot's face, who would be a terrorist. I imagined us looking at each other in the eyes when the nose of the plane was one millimetre from the building.
>
> I hate you, my eyes would tell him.
>
> I hate you, his eyes would tell me.

Here, the child narrator allows a repetition of the core idea of George W. Bush's 'Axis of Evil' rhetoric with no deeper attempt at engagement with the wider issues. The choice of the boy's name, in this novel, clearly echoes another child narrator, Oscar Matzerath from Günter Grass's *The Tin Drum* (1959): however, where Grass's child narrator enables a complex engagement with the rise of Nazism, Foer's doesn't engage with the complexities of 9/11 or the 'war on terror' and seems to rest on childish simplicities which have a dangerous political overtone.

Foer is a novelist whose work pushes at the boundaries of the form, characteristic of the fiction 'after postmodernism' that I discussed in Chapter 2, and he plays with the traditional form of the novel: it has—like Sebald, like Hemon—photographs, blank pages, it experiments with different forms and colours of text and print. But oddly these experiments highlight the same lack of engagement as the child narrator. For example, at a crucial revelatory moment in the text the lines get closer and closer together, and then overlap, so in the end one is left only with an inky illegible mess. The revelation is literally lost in or under the text. Later, the protagonist encodes the 'sum of his life' into three pages of text messaging numbers (which—try decoding it—become indeterminate pretty soon). Finally, the book ends wordlessly with the last pages given over to the famous shots of a man falling or jumping from the World Trade Center. These are presented like a child's flip book: as you flip them you discover that (ta dah, happy ending) the man falls upwards. The closing passage, just before the pictures, does a similar trick, unfalling Oskar's father, ungetting him to work in the Twin Towers, unwaking him up and so on. The conclusion? 'We would have been safe.' All these experiments—although I like the inky mess one—serve only to reinforce a sort of childishness which, rather than being a strategy for engaging with terrorism, seems to be a strategy for avoiding such an engagement.

Another strategy aimed at engaging with the issues raised by terrorism lies in Mohsin Hamid's *The Reluctant Fundamentalist* (2007). This short novel is one side of a conversation between two men: Changez, a Pakistani who has lived, studied, and worked in America, and a white, unnamed American listener, who might be a CIA operative, who may possibly have been sent to kill Changez. Similarly, Changez might be an assassin sent to kill, or at least assist in the killing of, the American. In order to entertain his listener, or perhaps to keep him there until further murderous accomplices arrive, Changez tells the story of his life, of his 'changes' (the names in this novel are meaningful). Having studied at Princeton, Changez took a Wall Street job with a firm called Underwood Samson: the initials significantly US, and the name displays a sense of strength (Sampson), American-ness (Sam's son) as well as something sinister, hidden, 'under wood' (under hand). The 'guiding principle' of this firm of financial pirates is 'focus on the fundamentals'. This is a clue that the novel is purposely unclear as to which 'fundamentalism'—religious, capitalistic—Changez is reluctant about. He also tells the story

of how he fell in love with an American woman, Erica
(again, something of the allegory here—Am-Erica), who is
mourning the love of her life, taken by cancer, Chris (perhaps
Chris(t)? or perhaps Christopher Columbus, as a symbol of a 'real'
America). Yet all is not well with Changez as he finds himself
between two worlds, his 'own identity…fragile': on a business trip
to the Philippines he tries to be more American, and yet this only
succeeds in making him realize how 'foreign' the native-born
Americans are. And it is in the Philippines where they hear of
the 9/11 attacks. Changez says that at:

> that moment, my thoughts were not with the victims of the attack…
> no, I was caught up in the symbolism of it all, the fact that someone
> had so visibly brought America to her knees. Ah, I see I am only
> compounding your displeasure…It is hateful to hear another
> person gloat over one's country's misfortune. But surely you cannot
> be completely innocent of such feelings yourself? Do you feel no joy
> at the video clips—so prevalent these days—of American munitions
> laying waste to the structures of your enemies?

The issue of the symbolism is very important. After 9/11, Changez,
for all his huge salary, is treated differently. He becomes the victim
of racist taunts and attacks. And while the United States
demonstrates its force in Afghanistan, Erica wastes away, ill and
full of sadness for Chris. On a work trip to Santiago, where the
firm is to value and so destroy a publishing company, Changez
encounters a Borges-like old publisher, Juan-Bautista, who tells
him of the Janissaries, the Christian soldiers who, taken as boys,
fought for the Ottoman Empire. This insightful suggestion leads
Changez to realize that:

> I was a modern day janissary, a servant of the American empire at a
> time when it was invading a country with a kinship to mine and was
> perhaps even colluding to ensure that my own country faced the
> threat of war. Of course I was struggling! Of course I felt torn! I had
> thrown in my lot with the men of Underwood Samson, with the

officers of empire, when all along I was predisposed to feel
compassion for those, like Juan-Bautista, whose lives the empire
thought nothing of overturning for its own gain.

He flees his work and returns to Pakistan, where he becomes a
radical critic of America and possibly a target for assassination
himself:

> It seemed to me then—and to be honest, sir, seems to me still—that
> America was engaged only in posturing. As a society, you were
> unwilling to reflect upon the shared pain that united you with those
> who attacked you. You retreated into myths of your own difference,
> assumptions of your own superiority. And you acted out these
> beliefs on the stage of the world, so that the entire planet was
> rocked by the repercussions of your tantrums, not least my family,
> now facing war thousands of miles away.

The names and the interest in symbolism show that this novel
is a modern allegory about American power, about the changes
that this wreaks on people.

The book isn't simply 'anti-American'. The processes of
globalization and the world of 'endless war' make this much too
simple. The conversation, its central conceit, is focused on the
American listener, and so, by proxy, aimed at an American reading
audience, written in English. Changez, on his return to Pakistan,
teaches the analytical skills he learned at Underwood Samson and
tells his interlocutor that he feels like 'a Kurtz waiting for a
Marlow', that is, the agent of empire at the 'Heart of Darkness'
awaiting his doom. It is the very 'America-ness' of the novel, and of
Changez, that allows its critique of America to work. The worlds
and the identities of Changez and the American listener are
inescapably bound up together. Moreover, just as *Shalimar the
Clown* finishes without ending, so this novel leaves everything
ambiguous. Perhaps the American is an assassin, perhaps Changez
is, but there are no clear answers provided here, no resolution.

Ian McEwan's 'all in one day' novel *Saturday* (2005) is set far away from Pakistan or New York and yet is centrally about them because it is about how the new global reach of terror erupts into everyday life and threatens to make each of us superfluous. Indeed, one of the reasons the novel was roundly criticized—the presentation of the comfy upper-middle-class existence of its protagonists—is precisely the point. Even the smugger, well-protected rich of the world are at risk from the way that terror 'breaks in' to their domestic lives. The protagonist is a successful brain surgeon, Henry Perowne, who lives with his wife, a lawyer, and two grown-up children, one a poet, the other a musician, in central London. He is a practical man with little time for things outside his narrow framework which focuses on the material world, doesn't see the point of art or literature (although, in his daughter's poem based on watching him work he sees 'art's essential but—he had to suppose—forgivable dishonesty'), and thinks religion foolish. The Saturday of the title is 15 February 2003, the day of a huge march through London against the incipient war in Iraq. Perowne wakes very early, and sees a plane on fire over London, which—combined with the march—leads his thoughts repeatedly to 9/11 and the 'war on terror'. On his way to play squash later in the morning, his car bumps that of a thug, Baxter (deprived of a first name) and there is an altercation. Perowne avoids being beaten up by diagnosing Baxter's medical condition, a degenerative genetic condition called Huntington's disease. (This disease has the slightest allegorical spin, too: the book *The Clash of Civilizations* (1996) by the American Samuel Huntington was often invoked in the 'war on terror'. In part by ignoring the sort of complexities Salman Rushdie and Mohsin Hamid point to, it suggests that there will be war between what it sees as the major world civilizations.) Much later in the day during a family meal, Baxter and his cronies break into Perowne's home. Baxter, a white British working-class criminal, is clearly a proxy for 'terrorism' (for Saddam Hussein, Osama Bin Laden, the anti-war demonstration, terrorism, endless war: in short anything that disrupts Henry Perowne's organized life). Baxter assaults the family and threatens to rape Daisy, the poet daughter. He makes her recite some of her work but she instead chooses to recall from memory Matthew Arnold's poem 'Dover Beach'. This distracts him ('It's beautiful. You know that, don't you? It's beautiful. And you wrote it.') and this allows Perowne and his son to get the better of Baxter and eventually hospitalize him. This moment of distraction is taken by some to be a moment of 'secular transcendence' in the novel, but in fact it's rather a simple ruse: a dog rushing in or a shout in the street would have done just as well as a distraction. Perowne eventually operates on Baxter and his life is saved, although Perowne is left feeling uneasy. Just as *The White Tiger* is about the global poor, this novel is about the impact of the world on the domestic life of the global rich.

In each of these novels there's an overwhelming sense that art, when faced with powerful violence, is a failure: it's the same experience as Diaz's Oscar. In *Saturday*, not only has Perowne no time for literature (as it is ridiculous) but also it serves only as a plot device to distract the invader. In the allegorical world of *The Reluctant Fundamentalist* Erica's writing withers away and dies with her and the Wall Street firm destroys the old Sanitago publisher. The childlike narrative approach of *Extremely Loud and Incredibly Close* fails to do justice to the complexity of the events. More, at the crux of a crucial subplot concerning Oskar's grandfather and his survival of the Dresden bombing in the Second World War, the text itself overlays words on words, as if many pages were typed on one page, making it impossible to read: literally the story of this terrible bombing cannot be told. Most clearly, in *Shalimar the Clown*, when the village in Kashmir is utterly destroyed, language and narrative are not competent to describe the events. A prophet from Shalimar's village, Pachigam, says that 'what's coming is so terrible that no prophet will have the words to foretell it' and sure enough, when the Indian army destroys the village it's clear that 'stories were stories and real life was real life, naked, ugly and finally impossible to cosmeticise in the greasepaint of a tale'. The terrible destruction of the village of

Pachigam is summed up three times. While it 'still exists' on official maps, this is the only memorial:

> [what] happened that day…need not be set down here in full detail, because brutality is brutality and excess is excess and that's all there is to it. There are things that must be looked at indirectly because they would blind you if you looked them in the face, like the fire of the sun. So to repeat: there was no Pachigam any more. Pachigam was destroyed. Imagine it for yourself.

> Second attempt: the village of Pachigam still existed on maps of Kashmir, but that day it ceased to exist anywhere else, except in memory.

> Third and final attempt: the beautiful village of Pachigam still exists.

The very rhetoric of these attempts, and the final collapse of Pachigam into an existence that is solely textual, marked only in a map and in a guidebook, reveals simply the inability of the text to enunciate the terror. And yet. What also remains of the fictional Pachigam, a version of the real villages destroyed in conflict, is the story of its destruction in a novel. While the strategies in all these novels seem to fail in some way in their engagement with terror, their very existence seems to mark a space in which something is held and maintained. This does not prevent human suffering, or the evil by which people are made superfluous, but does draw a special attention to it. This, it seems to me, is a new humility and a new way in which the novel aims to find a role.

Attention and superfluousness

This sense that the novel draws attention to those ways in which our lives are not superfluous is not only evoked as an overt response to terror, but exists in more subtle and pervasive forms. In this final section, I want to contrast two very different novels, both of which approach questions of superfluousness by thinking about what life means in the face of death. Frank

Kermode argued in his book *The Sense of an Ending* (1967) that fictions of all sorts were ways of coming to terms with our own deaths: their movement towards closure and the meaning that this created in them were models for our own lives, our own movement towards death and the ways in which we create meaning for ourselves in our own life. This is one of the reasons why the novel as a form has always had a slightly difficult relationship with religion or to other forms of transcendence which give life meaning: the novel, which arose as a secular form in the great move to secularism in the West, has always been too aware about how meaning in life is created. It displays, as it were, the narrative mechanism through which this happens, which leaves it, and its readers, slightly cynical (or at least better informed) about other, often more ancient, ways of creating meaning. Yet the two novels I want to look at here deal precisely with this, with the effect of transcendent ways of making death, and so life, intelligible in an age in which the risk is that all human life is made superfluous, redundant, and meaningless.

Jim Crace's *Being Dead* (1999) is a meditation on nature, death, and mourning. Early on in the novel, a 'quivering' is described: a fictional 19th-century custom, in which friends and family of the dead would loudly weep and bang things, then shake—'quiver'— the bed on which the dead lay, and then reminisce about them until dawn. Death, then, was not covered up but 'cultivated, like a plant'. The novel focuses on death. It is the story of an old married couple, Joseph and Celice, both zoologists, who return for a day to the long beach on which they first met as young research students. One strand of the novel describes this past: their meeting, courtship, and the death by fire of one of their peers. They visit the site of the destroyed research station where she died: 'this was not a haunted place, as it turned out. The studyhouse was fertile ground for rock shrubs and carbon-loving plants ... the last remains of bricks, masonry and walls were colonised by nettles, brambles, buddleia and mortar roses.'

Death here is a moment of transformation, part of a cycle. Making love, later, on the beach, the couple are murdered by a passing thief. The novel describes in great (but imagined) detail how the bodies become prey for insects and animals, and begin to rejoin the ecosystem of the dunes on which they lie, until their corpses are found by the police. The final strand of the novel concerns their disaffected daughter, Syl, who comes to find her missing parents. At the site of the murder, she is 'haunted and delighted' by the sight of 'her father's hand wrapped around her mother's leg'. It is an image that echoes Philip Larkin's famous (and uncharacteristically sentimental) poem 'An Arundel Tomb', in which the medieval effigies of an earl and his wife are holding hands, and it stands for the ways in which love survives death, in the form of children as the products of love and sex. Syl is also moved by her discovery that her parents have kept her baby teeth out of love for her. Yet the novel rejects any sense of an afterlife: the histories of Joseph and Celice 'were certain. No more to come…Nothing could be changed or mended, except by the sentiment and myth of those who were not dead. That's the only judgement day there is.' Indeed, the novel goes further. In describing the funeral service, the novel suggests that 'love songs transcend, transport, because there's such a thing as love. But hymns and prayers have feeble tunes because there are no gods.' The novel seems to offer no consolation in the face of death, outside the natural world's endless cycle: 'Syl…was too young to need the death-defying trick of living in a godless and expanding universe…Life is. It goes. It does not count. That was the hurtling truth that comes to rattle everyone as they grow up, grow old.' The role of the natural world, the cycle of life and meaning it appears to give in just its existence, and in transitory moments of love, seems to be the way that this novel responds to the threat of superfluousness. Yet in addition to these comforts, the penultimate chapter begins: 'So this has been a quivering of sorts for Joseph and Celice.' The 'this' here means the novel: the novel may not be offering much in the way of transcendence, but it does offer itself, a little retelling, the special attention to namelessness that the novel can give. The novel, the noise and the remembering by the living, its very attention, is the consolation.

Marilynne Robinson's astonishing and moving novel *Gilead* (2004) deals with the same issues in ways which both differ from and parallel Crace's work. Set in 1957, in Gilead, a small town in Iowa, it is ostensibly a letter from an ageing and ailing clergyman, John Ames, to his seven-year-old son, the child of his much younger wife. Where Crace's novel is godless, *Gilead* is profoundly religious, but it is neither dogmatic ('[T]he Lord absolutely transcends any understanding I have of Him, which makes loyalty to Him a different thing from loyalty to whatever customs and doctrines and memories I happen to associate with Him,' writes the protagonist) nor defensive ('nothing true can be said about God from a posture of defence'). While Ames, as an elderly man, does think a lot about heaven, the novel does not postulate redemption through this. Rather, and like Crace, it counters the sense of superfluousness through the ways in which Ames endows his every experience with an intense, and often joyful, thoughtfulness. This is true of the natural world:

> As I was walking up to the church this morning, I passed that row of big oaks...and I thought of another morning, fall a year or two ago, when they were dropping their acorns thick as hail almost. There was all sorts of thrashing in their leaves and there were acorns hitting the pavement so hard they'd fly past my head...It was a very clear night, or morning, very still, and then there was such energy in the things transpiring among those trees, like a storm, like travail. I stood a little out of range, and I thought, it is all still new to me. I have lived all my life on the prairie and a line of oak trees can still astonish me.

And again:

> I love the prairie! So often I have seen the dawn come and the light flood over the land and everything turn radiant at once, that word

'good' so profoundly affirmed in my soul that I am amazed I should be allowed to witness such a thing.

It is also true of language:

> The twinkling of an eye. That is the most wonderful expression. I've thought from time to time that it was the best thing in life, that little incandescence you see in people when the charm of a thing strikes them, or the humour of it.

And also, perhaps most importantly, of people: at a baptism, he is aware of the 'stern amazement' on his wife's face; he pays attention to his son's seriousness. He reflects on conversations gone wrong with his congregation from years before, turning the words in his mind.

But he is also, most of all, thoughtful about his own flaws: his failings, small ('I am also inclined to overuse the word old'), beyond his control (his age and his poverty), and large: his anger, jealousy, and occasional dislike of people. The novel is also about people's flaws, and especially the flawed relationships between fathers and sons. Both Ames's father and grandfather were clergymen, but his grandfather had fought as an abolitionist in the Civil War and had lost an eye fighting, while his father was a pacifist: Ames recalls a confrontation between them, his father saying to his grandfather:

> 'I remember when you walked to the pulpit in that shot-up, bloody shirt with that pistol in your belt. And I had a thought as powerful and clear as any revelation. And it was, This has nothing to do with Jesus. Nothing. Nothing.'

Similarly, Ames's father makes a remark to Ames which makes him feel as if 'a great cold wind swept over me' and creates a break between them. Even more significantly, Ames's best friend, Broughton, has a son, Jack, who had left Gilead after scandalously fathering a child without marrying the mother but returns during the time of the novel. He and his father, and he and Ames, have very difficult relationships. Ames is jealous of Jack's closeness with his own young wife, and thinks hard and long, and not always clearly, about his feelings. However, Jack's flaws turn out to be involved in the wider national flaws which historically bookend the novel: the Civil War and the beginnings of the Civil Rights movement. Jack asks Ames if he ever wonders 'why American Christianity always seems to wait for the real thinking to be done elsewhere?': the unspoken answer is that there is, in 1957, a blindness to issues of race. Yet the core of this novel is the way in which religion engenders a thoughtfulness and attention which give a meaning to each life, however small or flawed, and answers the fear characteristic of the present that each of us is redundant. For Robinson, the answer lies not in doctrines or promises but in the very acts of attention to and care for others. And this novel itself enacts that attention which is its subject.

Unique and Singular

I've looked at the ways in which contemporary fiction engages explicitly with the present and what 'everyone knows' the issues of the day are (although what 'everyone knows' can be wrong: who with utter confidence would be prepared to say that the historians of the future, if there is to be a future, would not find some other meanings or shapes to our age?). Against the risk that globalization and terror, as well as the other problems of our time, make human beings as human beings superfluous, the novel as an art form doesn't offer much. It won't stop global warming, nor will it prevent torturers from maiming or killing their victims. Individual writers might take more political action, found charities, and so on, but writing itself seems weak. One of the characteristics of contemporary fiction, for all its ability to analyse or obscure, complicate or simplify, for all the strategies novelists employ, seems to be a recognition of this: 'brutality is brutality and excess is excess and that's all there is to it'. Thus, a new humility in fiction. In the face of the world, in the face of each of our deaths, in this humility lies a renewed if limited sense of what the novel can do (if it chooses to, it needn't do anything, it's a strange institution than can say anything). In the present it can draw attention to the wonders of the everyday, to our flaws and the flaws of others, to our hopes. It can point out and in its prose enact and make intelligible the significance of our brief, finite, utterly unique, and singular lives.

Chapter 6
The future

The previous chapters have covered how the contemporary novel deals with the past and the present: this one turns, naturally enough, to the future. The image of the future in contemporary fiction is entirely entangled with ideas about the impact of technology: expressions of hope or despair about that future are measured through the figure of the child.

In our daily lives, in the developed and developing world, we use the Internet, smartphones, Facebook, Twitter: a whole panoply of contemporary new technologies that didn't exist twenty or even ten years ago. The rate of change and development is so fast that between my writing these words, now, here, and your reading them, whenever that is, there will have been significant technological changes. One of the features of the contemporary age is this pressure and speed of change. Our visions of the future are shaped by this constant novelty—its continuation or its (often sudden) absence, through some technological Armageddon. And this newness is linked to the novel: the word 'novel' means 'new'. When the novel began in the 18th century it was 'new' with new subjects for storytelling (ordinary people, living more or less ordinary lives, not mythic heroes or iconic figures) with new ways or forms through which to tell those stories. It was supported by new technologies: innovative printing and publishing practices, mass production, faster wide distribution. As a commercial and successful form of writing, the novel has always been connected to innovations in technology—cheaper paper and paperback binding in the 1930s, for example; the Kindle and various forms of e-reading now. The institution of the novel-as-business loves technological change: but how do novels themselves deal with contemporary technology?

I asked (on Facebook and Twitter) for suggestions for some novels written since 2000 that did feature contemporary technology and I had only a few suggestions: David Lodge's *Thinks* (2001); Don DeLillo's *Cosmopolis* (2003); Margaret Atwood's speculative fictions *Oryx and Crake* (2003) and *The Year of the Flood* (2009); Jonathan Lethem's *Chronic City* (2009); Tom McCarthy's *C* (2010); Gary Shteyngart's *Super Sad True Love Story* (2010). *A Week in December* (2009) by Sebastian Faulks has satirical representations of social networking. Ali Smith's *The Accidental* features mobile phones and the Internet. But oddly, given that technology is so much a part of our lives, there seems to be rather a dearth of fiction that deals with it directly. Partially, this is because novels take time to gestate, to be written, and to be published, and the rate of change is so fast that it has swamped this process. But this is rather too simple a view of technology—that technology is 'just gadgets'. There is a more complex reason. Because technology is central to our culture (and to the very existence of the novel as an art form) it's actually quite hard to see: the essence of technology is too close to us, like the glasses we forget we're wearing and then go to look for.

The essential thing about technology is that, despite our iPhones and computers and digital cameras and constant change, it is not new at all. In fact, human civilization over the longest possible time grew up not just hand in hand with technology but *because* of technology. Technology isn't just something added to 'being human' the way we might acquire another gadget: the essence of technology is in the creation of tools, technology in the creation of farming and in buildings, cities, roads, and machines.

And perhaps the most important form of technology is right here in front of you, you're looking at it right now, this second: writing. It too—these very letters here, now—is, of course, a technology. Writing is a 'machine' to supplement both the fallible and limited nature of our memory (it stores information over time) and our bodies over space (it carries information over distances). So it's not so much that we humans made technology: *technology also made us*. As we write, so writing makes us. It is technology that allows us history, as a recorded past and so a present, and so, perhaps a future. So to think about technology, and changes in technology, is to think about the very core of what we, as a species, are and about how we are changing. As we change technology, we change ourselves. And all novels, because they are a form of technology, implicitly or explicitly, do this.

The word 'technology' comes from the Greek word 'techne': techne is the skill of the craftsman or woman at building things (ships, tables, tapestries) but also, interestingly, the skill of crafting art and poetry. 'Techne' is the skill of seeing how, say, these pieces of wood would make a good table if sanded and used in just that way, or seeing the shape of David in the block of marble, or in hearing how these phrases will best represent the sadness you imagine Queen Hecuba feels in mourning her husband and sons. It's also the skill, in our age, of working out how best to use resources to eliminate a disease globally, or to deliver high-quality education. But 'techne' has become more than just skill: it is a whole *way of thinking* about the world. In this 'technological thinking', everything in the world is turned into a potential resource for use, everything is a tool for doing something. Rocks become sources of ore; trees become potential timber for carpentry or pulp for paper; the wind itself is captured by a windmill or, in a more contemporary idiom, 'farmed' in a wind farm. Companies have departments of 'human resources'. Even an undeveloped piece of natural land, purposely left undisturbed by buildings and agriculture, becomes a 'wilderness park', a 'machine' in which to relax and recharge oneself from the strains of everyday life. Great works of literature are turned into a resource through which to measure people, by exams or in quizzes. This is the point of the old saw, 'To a man with a hammer, everything looks like a nail': to a technological way of thinking, everything looks like a resource to be used (just as to a carpenter, all trees look like potential timber; to a university academic, all fiction is a source of exam questions). More than this, the modern networks which use these resources are bigger and more complex. Where once the windmill ground the miller's corn to make bread, now a huge global food system moves food resources about internationally: understanding and using these networks are a career in themselves. This technological thinking, rather than the tools it produces, is a taken-for-granted 'framework' in which we come to see and understand everything. Although many people have made this sort of observation about the world, the influential and contentious German philosopher Martin Heidegger, from whom much of the above is drawn, made it most keenly.

Is this a bad thing? It certainly sounds as if it might be. Who wants, after all, to be seen only as a 'human resource'? It's precisely technological thinking that has put the world at risk of total destruction. On the other hand, technology has offered so much to so many: in curing illness and alleviating pain, for example. The question is too big to answer in these simple terms of 'bad' or 'good'. However, contemporary fiction seems very negative about technology, positing dystopias and awful ends for humanity. However, I want to suggest that contemporary fiction doesn't find the world utterly without hope, precisely because of technology.

Three levels of technology

With these ideas about the essence of technology in mind, I want to make some distinctions about how contemporary fiction 'thinks' about technology. First, of course, are the novels set in the contemporary period that use technology, that feature the recognizable technologies of the second decade of the third millennium, things many of us use every day: technology as gadgets. At a second level are those that seem to engage more deeply with technology, to explore what it means to think technologically and what the consequences of this are. And finally, we can look at novels that take the idea of 'writing as technology' seriously and reflect on this: after all, we pass over the idea of 'writing as a machine' so very easily, but it still comes as a shock to me, every time, when I try and focus on what this might actually mean. Each of these, too, has a different use of the idea of the child, the inchoate figure of future hope or despair.

Jennifer Egan's *A Visit from the Goon Squad* (2010) features technological devices and is about how we use recent technology. (Technology is a fascination of hers: in the summer of 2012, she wrote a rather gripping story solely on Twitter, using the shortness of the tweets to great narrative effect.) This novel, like several other successful contemporary novels (see Chapter 2), is made up of many interconnected stories over a span just longer than a generation, the 1970s to the 2020s: the children in one story are parents in another, and so on. Most of the characters are involved in the music or media business. The 'goon squad' of the title is the passing of time and the impact of this on all of the characters. The 'ensemble cast' age and face large and small existential crises in a range of different styles and formats. One of these stories, from the 2020s, is told using a PowerPoint-like projection. The 'narrator' is the daughter of a family who live in the desert. Between her doctor father and her brother, Lincoln (who, we know from a previous story, is 'slightly autistic'), there is a tension. Lincoln is obsessed with pauses in pop songs and finds in this obsession the only way to communicate with his father. His father just doesn't understand this. The story is told via PowerPoint because this seems the only way the daughter can make her point: asked by her mother if she wouldn't rather write a 'proper' journal entry, she replies with phrases like 'A word-wall is a long haul!'

and 'give us the issues not the tissues!'. The presentation tells how, during a night-time walk with his daughter, the father learns to appreciate the son. Despite the amusing and rather moving PowerPoint presentation here, there is nothing that the technology offers that is new in terms of form: the story is told differently, but the core of it—'daughter helps father appreciate son'—isn't new and could have been told in more conventional realist prose. The story also seems heart-warming about the relationship between the generations, and the children thrive.

The final chapter in *A Visit from the Goon Squad*, again set in the near future, concerns several of the characters from the book: Bennie, a music promoter; Scott, a failed musician; and Alex, a man with a young family who needs a job. In this future, hand-held 'pointer' devices, the descendents of smartphones, are ubiquitous: even small children have them. Bennie tries to persuade the out-of-work Alex to become a 'parrot', to spread 'word of mouth' advertising about music on his pointer as if it was his own opinion: it's 'not about music. It's about reach,' says Bennie. Alex's worry is that there is something 'inherently wrong with believing in something—or saying you do—for money'. Despite his concerns, through his 'parroting' a huge crowd is assembled for Scott's 'comeback' gig:

'He's supposed to be really good live,' said Natasha...

'I heard that, too,' Rebecca said. 'From, like, eight different people. It's almost strange.'

'Not strange,' Natasha said, with a harsh laugh. 'People are getting paid.' Alex felt a blaze of heat in his face and found it hard to look at Natasha...

'But these are people I know,' Rebecca said.

The technology and the desire to make money have combined to make Alex ashamed of himself. Backstage, Scott is too nervous to go on, feeling too old, but Bennie is persuading him: 'Time's a goon, right?...You gonna let a goon push you around?' and eventually Scott goes on stage. But here an odd thing happens: the gig is a huge success precisely because Scott is so unaffected by technology. He plays songs 'ripped off the chest of a man you know just by looking has never has a page or a profile or a handle or a handset, who was part of no one's data, a guy who had lived in the cracks all these years, unforgotten and full of rage, in a way that now registered as pure. Untouched.' Here, the authenticity of Scott and the shameful blush of Alex—which reveals that for all his 'parroting' on his pointer, he still has a moral compass of sorts—puncture the seemingly all-powerful technology and seem, in this novel, to be a form of hope in a humanity uncorrupted by technology, not simply turned into a superfluous resource. This also echoes the importance of silences for both the autistic Lincoln and his father: the point of the silences is that however much one records them, they escape the grasp of technology because there is literally nothing there in the recording technology. Lincoln and his father listen to what is not there, and so hear themselves.

However, I wonder if this novel is not rather too optimistic about the limits of technology and a sense of humanity beyond it. For all the power of the 'pointers', often in the hands of infants, of the amusing examples of text speak (txtspk) Egan offers, and the story told via PowerPoint, these are examples of the impact of *pieces* of technology. Children still live on as children and become adults; the future seems roughly the same as now. The novel is concerned with the passage of time, moral choices, with family relations, and doesn't investigate the impact of what I've called 'technological thinking'.

While still concerned with moral choices and with family (the central image is of a girl dancing with a baby doll, pretending to be a mother) Kazuo Ishiguro's profoundly moving novel *Never Let Me Go* (2005) is much, much more pessimistic and more frightening. Yet, because of the lightness of touch, and the passive, calming temperament of the central character, Kathy H—the novel is told in the first person—this darkness seeps into rather than overwhelms the novel and lasts in its 'after-reading' (the way a novel stays with the reader for some time after the last page is read). All Ishiguro's work concerns the complex historical knotting between the individual and wider society, especially when that society is deeply morally compromised. He traces how these collective flaws and corrupted histories are filtered down and through the central characters in his novels. *Never Let Me Go* is slightly different in that it concerns someone not centrally an actor in this corruption but rather its victim. Set in 'England, late 1990s', it begins:

> My name is Kathy H. I'm thirty-one years old, and I've been a carer now for over eleven years. That sounds long enough I know, but actually they want me to go on for another eight months, until the end of this year.

The 'H' is significant: why has she not got a full name? The single letter reminds us both of those characters in Kafka ('K') trapped in frightening mad-yet-recognizable worlds, and also of a 'batch' number. More than this, the term 'carer' seems to be more than simply a job description, and indeed, terms like 'carer' and 'donor' (and later 'student') are being used in a slightly angled way: they have, it will emerge in the world of this novel, a very specific and euphemistic meaning. The 'they' too sounds odd, especially when contrasted with the informal and conversational tags 'I know' and the 'until the end of the year': it fixes us, the reader, as someone in conversation with Kathy, with fixed points that we do know (it must be April when she is talking to us, for example, 'another eight months, until the end of this year') and fixed points that we are *supposed* to know, but don't. Kathy H clearly assumes that we know what 'long enough' means ('long enough' for what?) and who 'they' are. We are made, as it were, complicit with something that we don't yet understand.

Kathy goes on to describe her upbringing in a rather posh school called Hailsham. The students don't seem to have that many lessons, except art, and the teachers are called 'guardians', another euphemism. One guardian tells Kathy's school mate Tommy that they aren't being taught enough: what 'she was talking about was, you know, about us, about what's going to happen to us one day. Donations and all that.' 'But we have been taught about all that,' replies Kathy. It slowly dawns on the reader as the novel develops that Kathy, Tommy, and all their friends are clones. They exist only to be harvested for their organs ('donations', but not really gifts at all: another angled word). In an efficient twist, those yet to be harvested are carers for the dying clones. We are hearing the voice, basically, of a piece of technology, a human clone with feelings, desires, fears, character—a person—who is to be used and then thrown away. A retired guardian tells Kathy:

> You must try and see it historically. After the war, in the early fifties, when the great breakthroughs in science followed one after the other so rapidly, there wasn't time to take stock, to ask the sensible questions. Suddenly there were all these new possibilities laid before us, all these new ways to cure previously incurable conditions... And for a long time, people preferred to believe that these organs appeared from nowhere, or at most they were grown in some kind of a vacuum. Yes there were arguments. But by the time people became concerned about... about *students*... well by then it was too late... How can you ask a world that has come to regard cancer as curable, how can you ask such a world to put away that cure to go back to the dark days?... However uncomfortable people were about your existence, their overwhelming concern was that their own children, their spouses, their parents, their friends, did not die from cancer, motor neurone disease, heart disease.

In Hailsham, the students are encouraged to produce art, because—the retired guardian again—'your art will reveal your inner selves... because your art will reveal your souls!' This seeming revelatory art was used in the 'arguments' to prove that the clones were near human, should be treated better, and so on: yet it had no effect, of course. Kathy and her friends are trapped, not by guards or fences but simply by the universal acceptance of this 'technological thinking'. They will be murdered for their body parts. There is no resistance and no hope of salvation for them. Tommy, as a child and as an adult, has terrible temper tantrums, expressing his unconscious anger: Kathy is simply more accepting and exhibits an impressive self-control. Her 'escapes' are in moments of imagination: dancing with a doll to a pop song; a 'little fantasy' on the final page of the novel. Unlike *A Visit from the Goon Squad*, this novel doesn't offer something like an authentic moment of humanity that shines through the imposition of technology. Here, 'technological thinking' has utterly and completely taken over what it is to be human, but so gently that we hardly notice. And, just as the first sentences of the novel show, it has made us, the readers, complicit with this. We don't even notice the technological 'frame' which has done this. Perhaps it serves to remind us of how much, in our non-fictional world, we take versions of this for granted: how, as the great German critic Walter Benjamin wrote, there 'is no document of civilization which is not at the same time a document of barbarism'.

The central image is that of Kathy dancing by herself to a song called 'Never Let Me Go' while cradling a doll:

> I'd imagine ... a woman who'd been told she couldn't have children, who'd really really wanted them all her life. Then there's a sort of miracle and she has a baby, and she holds this baby very close to her and walks around singing 'Baby, never let me go ...' partly because she's so happy, but also because she's afraid that something will happen, that the baby will get ill or be taken away from her.

Kathy will never be allowed to have children, indeed, may have been manufactured to be unable to have children. The child is both herself, not real, and her own hopes for her future: barren and futile, unexpressed except in this moment. The lack of hope in the future for the clones, expressed in this piteous maternal image, is precisely the result of the quite human love for people's own children, spouses, parents, and friends. In this way, through love, a hope in technology has been turned utterly to evil.

To these two judgements on technology—the one optimistic, suggesting that something human and 'untouched' escapes it and the future thrives; the other pessimistic, exploring the corrupting and murderous power of technological thinking—it is possible to add a third. As I suggested earlier, in ancient Greek, 'techne' is not only the skill of making things with tools, but also the skill of making art and poetry (indeed, 'poeisis', the source of our word 'poetry', means 'making'). Heidegger makes much of this: where he sees great danger in 'technological thinking'—the sort of danger that *Never Let Me Go* explores so quietly and yet so powerfully—he also sees what he calls a 'saving power'. For Heidegger, it is through the 'techne' of art that the dangers to the world and to all of us created by technological thinking might be avoided or, at least, mitigated. Heidegger and this way of thinking about technology are inspired by the Romantic movement, by poets in Germany like Friedrich Hölderlin, and in Britain by William Wordsworth and John Clare. These poets tried, in the face of the Industrial Revolution, to explore a different relationship between ourselves and our world. Some critics, like Jonathan Bate, have suggested that these sorts of writers might be a way to help us stop or suspend our dominant 'technological thinking' precisely because they draw attention to our relation to the natural world. They stop and make us engage with nature, put us, however briefly, in 'tune' with it. In the UK, tourism to the Lake District, to look at the views that moved Wordsworth and others and be moved in our turn, is an echo of this. Conversely, the enforced 'appreciation' of nature, encouraged by guidebooks and tours, is a reminder of how easy it is for 'technological thinking' to turn anything into a resource—a machine for 'relaxing' us, a chance to sell postcards and knick-knacks. There are some contemporary writers, too, developing in this same Romantic mould, who are keen to use their experience of nature to draw our attention to both the natural world and our own thought: Robert MacFarlane's beautiful books *The Lonely Places* (2007) and *The Old Ways* (2012) are examples of this and of the sort of mixing of fiction and non-fiction, influenced by Sebald, that I discussed in Chapter 2.

However, it is precisely the idea of 'writing as technology' rather than a return to nature that plays a central role in the work of David Mitchell, one of the most successful and interesting of recent British novelists. His first novel *Ghostwritten* (1999) is, like Egan's, a story built from multiple strands and, as the title itself suggests, focuses attention on the act of writing itself. While his most recent novel, *The Thousand Autumns of Jacob de Zoet* (2010), deals with the relationship between Japan and the West, *Cloud Atlas* (2004) deals most explicitly with technology and with writing. An example of the sort of novel that comes after postmodernism but has retreated from the 'high tide' of experiment, it consists of six linked but different stories, each 'nestled inside the other' like Russian dolls. The first story, the journal of a lawyer, Adam Ewing, crossing the Pacific in the middle of the 19th century, is discovered by an unhappy young British composer in the 1930s; the composer's lover keeps the letters (they are 'what he would save from a burning building') and in the 1980s, he, in turn, is a character in a 1970s detective thriller, which, again in turn, is a manuscript read by Timothy Cavendish, the protagonist of the next story: *his* narrative is a film then watched by the novel's most moving character, a clone slave called Sonmi-451 from a future dystopia. Her recording of her story, in a device called an 'orison' (from *Hamlet*, 'the fair Ophelia! Nymph, in thy orisons be all my sins remember'd': 'orison' is an archaic word for 'prayer') is included in the central tale, set in a destroyed world in which humans have returned to a primitive state and in which Sonmi is regarded as a goddess: and this story itself is a retelling of a tale told by the narrator's father, Zachry. Each tale, except the final one which is in the middle of the novel, is interrupted by the previous tale, creating five different narrative cliffhangers in one single novel. Each is then resumed, and all of them are contained, like a fractal pattern, within the sin-remembering 'orison'. There are other similarities: each protagonist has a comet-shaped birthmark, each has a fall. And thematically they are linked because each one is the prey of an enemy throughout, yet each one, in different ways, undergoes a trial and emerges if not victorious (Sonmi-451 is executed, the composer commits suicide) then with integrity and more importantly, perhaps, with hope. The composer believes in one rather literal interpretation of Nietzsche's doctrine of the 'eternal return' and so hopes to return; Sonmi-451, unlike poor Kathy H, has circulated her ideas about the abolition of clone slavery in composing a revolutionary text called *Declarations* which she hopes will lead to change. Old Zachry in the final story says:

> Souls cross ages like clouds cross skies, an' tho' a cloud's shape nor hue nor size don't stay the same it's still a cloud an' so is a soul. Who can say where the cloud's blowed from or who the soul'll be 'morrow? Only Sonmi the east an' the west an' the compass an' the atlas, yas, only the atlas o'clouds. (324).

Indeed, the 'cloud atlas' also occurs in each story, but more importantly, it sets the idea for the transmutation of a soul. This transmutation of souls also stands for a sort of parentage, as each story seems to be a parent to the next. This is clearest in the central story, in which Somni is a sort of maternal goddess.

Even this very quick description of this bravura performance of a novel makes it clear how it revels in the very technology of writing itself. The cliffhangers caused by the 'nestling' chapters are models of the technology of suspense, one of the techniques that keeps people reading. The novel draws attention to the nature of writing as a machine, with the technologies of writing: journals, letters, manuscripts, tapes, futuristic recording devices, and the repetitions of primitive folk tales. The reader, unlike the characters, is the one to make the connections, finding parallels and transmuted links in a sort of self-conscious version of the normal technologies of reading. For example, the last pages record the decision of Adam Ewing to become an active abolitionist in the pre-Civil War United States, in an echo of Sonmi-451's own commitment to freedom; the novel begins and ends in voyages across the Pacific. The book is itself the record of this soul: the book is a cloud atlas, conveniently named *Cloud Atlas*.

But more than this, the novel draws attention to technology in general and writing in particular, and views them both as a danger and as a potential saving force. Metaphorically, this is shown in the way that the attainments of civilization are preserved by the still technologically advanced survivors Old Zachry meets, in the way that Sonmi-451's *Declarations* are circulated, or by the survival of the composer's love letters. But even more deeply, the core of the book's idea is about the coming together of 'technological thinking' and ethical thinking. The final pages of the novel declare Ewing's belief that there is no shape or hidden order to history (no 'metanarrative' which would explain and justify all the other narratives, as the French philosopher of postmodernism, Jean-Francois Lyotard, would put it). There are only outcomes that stem from 'vicious acts and virtuous acts' and these stem in turn from beliefs. Ewing writes, rather beautifully, that belief 'is both prize and battlefield, within the mind and in the mind's mirror, the word'. If we believe that humanity is simply one individual or community pitted against the other in a 'collosseum of confrontation, exploitation and bestiality' then 'such humanity is surely brought into being'. 'Is this,' writes Ewing, 'the entropy written within our nature?' The problem with this for Ewing is that this 'selfishness is extinction' for the whole species. Yet, Ewing continues, if we believe that we can as a species transcend this and that diverse 'races and creeds can share this world… peaceably… if we believe leaders must be just, violence muzzled, power accountable and the riches of the earth and its oceans shared equitably, such a world will come to pass'. This written argument is oddly a piece of 'technological thinking'. The reason to reduce suffering and to instil justice is not because these are good things in themselves but rather because they will ensure longer resources for all. Justice and hope are simply tools to ensure adequate resources (and there are lots of reasons to reject this idea, more even than Ewing makes clear: we might simply not believe that the resources are limited that way, or might not worry about something that won't happen until long after we are dead, or we might simply decide that it's someone else's problem). And yet in the artwork of *Cloud Atlas* we have a space to reflect on this moment where 'technological thinking' and the thinking of justice as it were 'outside' technology come together for an instant. The writing itself is this space or makes this space. *Cloud Atlas* finds in technology both the forms of endless predation and destruction and the forms by which something, perhaps very little, can be saved.

Conclusion

The future explored in contemporary fiction is usually pretty bleak. Cormac McCarthy's *The Road* (2006) presents a world entirely ruined where everything, even the fish of the sea, is dead or dying. Again, in this novel, the hope or despair is gauged in the figure of the child. Shteyngart's *Super Sad True Love Story*, which does engage with all sorts of technology, also concerns the relationships between parents and children. This measurement seems to occur throughout contemporary fiction and perhaps—whatever our feelings about children in our own lives—tells us something of the fears we as a species have for the future and what hope we invest in our children. And yet, as in the previous chapter, the moments of attention, the orison/'prayer', Kathy's telling of her story, are moments of hope.

Chapter 7

Conclusion: 'Hey everyone, look at that beautiful thing' / 'Yes, but...'

This book you are finishing is in the genre known as literary criticism. This genre is basically 'saying what you think about books' and in the 'strange institution' of literature there are lots of different people who do this for different reasons. For example, a leading literary agent in the spring of 2012—I've blanked out the name—tweeted: 'Proud day for [agency name] as our authors secure Number 1, 2 & 3 spot in this week's bestseller's pb chart'. This is a form of criticism: his thought about the books is a pride in their success as business products, and that's fair enough. But it isn't about the novels as novels. Similarly, journalists often cover the 'whole story' of an author, their feuds and heartbreaks, the human interest that accompanies a new novel. Again, that's criticism too, but it isn't really about the particular novel. Literary reviewers have to make speedy judgements about novels that have taken years to write. One consequence of this is that these critics often find a line they like about literature in general ('It should do this!') and stick to it. Instead of trying to attend to the novel as it is, they have to fit it into or reject it from their model of the world. (This also explains a phenomenon that has always mystified me in literary journalism, the certainty reviewers seem to have about novels: to be honest, it takes me ages and ages to work out what I really think about a book, and I often change my mind.) Oddly, then, lots of criticism seems to obscure or even ignore novels instead of illuminating them.

In this context, the role of the author, beyond being a 'brand' or selling point for a novel, is interesting. They are interviewed and questioned about their novels but, honestly, I find it hard to understand why. Surely—outside simple celebrity—it is the novel, not the novelist, which is the thing of interest? One of the longest debates in academic criticism—it's been going over sixty years—is over what's called 'authorial intention'. Roughly speaking, it's about how much weight a reader puts on what an author says their work means. On the one hand, there's a link between the word 'author' and 'authority' and it seems normal to assume that the author knows what they mean (that's an assumption we make in everyday speech, after all). On the other hand, whatever anyone says, each reader comes to their own conclusions about what a novel means, how much they enjoy it, and everyone makes their own interpretation. That's one of the reasons people love novels. There's something about reading—living through—a novel that makes it *yours* and this makes your opinion as good as the next person's. Moreover, if a novel really was simply a message from an author's brain to yours that could be easily summarized (saying sophisticated versions of 'War is bad' or 'Love hurts'), you wouldn't actually need to read the novel in the first place. In this view, an author is not the 'authority' on their work, simply a well-informed critic. Perhaps paying too much attention to what an author says about their work can get in the way of paying attention to the novel in the first place.

I'd like to say that university academics, critics, are different, but this is one of the things that John Ames's friend Boughton in *Gilead* would describe as 'the pulpit speaking'. The British author Geoff Dyer writes that university academic literary criticism 'kills everything it touches. Walk around a university campus and there is an almost palpable smell of death about the place because hundreds of academics are busy killing everything they touch.' He feels that the academic industry turns literature to dust and the dust is embalmed in publications about literature and, he writes, 'before you know it, literature is a vast graveyard of dust, a dustyard of graves... How could these people with no feeling for literature have ended up teaching it, writing about it?' The 'overwhelming majority of books by academics... are a crime against literature'. (To be fair, he does go on to say 'this is nonsense of course. Scholars live their works too... I withdraw that claim... unconditionally—but I also want to let it stand, conditionally.') Dyer's counterblast to murderous academic criticism is to write brilliant, clever, and funny 'imaginative criticism' that responds personally to literature and film, which usually tells the reader more about Dyer than about the artwork (but this, perhaps, just makes explicit what all criticism does).

What is the best way to do criticism, then? Perhaps there is none: David Eggers says that criticism:

> comes from the opposite place that book-enjoying should come from. To enjoy art one needs time, patience, and a generous heart, and criticism is done, by and large, by impatient people who have axes to grind. The worst sort of critics are (analogy coming) butterfly collectors—they chase something, ostensibly out of their search for beauty, then, once they get close, they catch that beautiful something, they kill it, they stick a pin through its abdomen, dissect it and label it. The whole process, I find, is not a happy or healthy one. Someone with his or her own shit figured out, without any emotional problems or bitterness or envy, instead of killing that which he loves, will simply let the goddamn butterfly fly, and instead of capturing and killing it and sticking it in a box, will simply point to it—'Hey everyone, look at that beautiful thing'—hoping everyone else will see the beautiful thing he has seen. Just as no one wants to grow up to be an IRS agent, no one should want to grow up to maliciously dissect books.

Yes, no child should want to grow up to maliciously dissect books. Yes, too, all criticism should *begin* with 'look at that beautiful thing', but I'm not sure that this is *all* criticism should be. Throughout this book I've talked about how novels 'think'.

They don't do this thinking in the same way as philosophy, with rigorous logic, trying to get from assertion P to assertion Q to assertion R, nor like a work of history, with evidence and references. Indeed, their 'thinking' can say anything and be in any form, and perhaps even 'thinking' is the wrong word: no definition seems to cover or properly explain what a work of literature is or does. But it seems to me that part of the joy and interest of literature is precisely this refusal of any definition. F. R. Leavis, a critic celebrated and castigated in near-equal amounts, thought that the ideal debate about literature was unending: to any proposition about a literary work, 'This is so, isn't it?' the response should be 'Yes, but…'. The first task of a critic of contemporary fiction is to follow and to try to understand the sinuous 'thinking' of a novel, its beauty, and to think themselves or with others the 'This is so', and then to answer, 'Yes, but…'.

The main reason why Leavis was castigated was because of the (correct) suspicion that his judgements about the literary value of some novels over others betrayed an unspoken ideology. One response to Leavis, among Dyer's morticians of literature in universities, was an attempt to deny not that this or that was a good novel, but to deny the importance of literary value itself. But this is nonsense. Just choosing to read or reread, or choosing to teach, any literary work over another is a judgement of literary value. And liking or not liking a novel just happens. If you find that you like a novel, it's interesting and perhaps important to find out why. You may not be able to explain fully, of course. Or the reasons might be autobiographical (your beloved grandfather read it to you) or political or anything else that isn't 'strictly literary'. But because 'strictly literary' is impossible to define, that's acceptable, it seems to me. However, the more demanding form of criticism means explaining to others why some novels seem more valuable to you and some less.

Criticism also means, I think, finding patterns. Finding patterns in fiction is a way in which we become intelligible to ourselves.

This book has tried to find patterns in some fiction: innovations in form, new ways of engaging with the past, a 'new humility' in fiction, a concern with technological thinking. But there are a near-infinite number of other patterns that could be drawn out. (For example, I have been very struck in writing this book how children seem to play a major role in many contemporary novels, including several I've discussed here: as protagonists in Ali Smith's fiction, victims in Salman Rushdie's and Ian McEwan's, as symbols of the future in Javier Cercas's novel. There's also a sort of childishness, playful and full of pathos in Eggers's first novel, slightly questionable in Foer's second. Is it the case that in the last ten years or so, years of fear and turmoil, children have become a new way of evading or expressing something as yet unclear?)

The novel, all forms of art in fact, needs not only creators but what Martin Heidegger calls 'preservers' too. People who write novels 'in the tradition of' or reproduce generic types of fiction fulfil this role, but so do critics. Critics help to make works intelligible and understood (although, Dyer might say, they also obscure and kill them). In the case of contemporary fiction, this is especially important. The novel is not dying as a form, but, in the clamour of newer art forms (cinema, TV, games, the Internet, pop music) as well as in the light of all that this book has discussed, it is constantly renegotiating its public role. A task of the critic is to help with this continual process.

And part of that process, and another task for a critic, lies in thinking about novels and the wider world. After his remark about the definition of literature, Derrida goes on to describe how:

> [the] institution of literature in the West, in its relatively modern form, is linked to an authorisation to say everything, and doubtless too to the coming about of the modern idea of democracy. Not that it depends on a democracy in place, but it seems inseparable to me from what calls forth a democracy, in the most open (and doubtless itself to come) sense of democracy.

Derrida puts a lot of weight on the idea of 'democracy to come'. For him it means a critique of the current world in the name of something to come. This means, oddly, that the 'democracy to come' is somehow already here in the present, it's where that critique comes from. He also takes it to mean an extension of human rights to people beyond simply the rights granted by citizenship of one state: a general rethinking of what 'we' means. He also means it as a call to justice and to think about justice. In the sense of 'to come', too, is something of what Arendt called 'spontaneity', the hopeful power to begin something anew. Contemporary fiction is linked to all this in ways yet to be more fully explored.

This book concerns how novels think, the patterns they make, their value and role in the world. I think novels in general, and especially the novels discussed, are beautiful and important, and I have said why. But no book about books really ends. The task of the reader, another critic, is to say: 'Yes, but ...'.

References

Chapter 1: Saying everything

Jacques Derrida, *Acts of Literature* ed. Derek Attridge (London: Routledge, 1992)

Chapter 2: Form, or, what's contemporary about contemporary fiction?

David Eggers, *A Heartbreaking Work of Staggering Genius* (New York: Simon and Schuster, 2000)

B. S. Johnson, *Aren't You Rather Young to Be Writing Your Memoirs?* (London: Hutchinson, 2005)

Frank Kermode, *The Sense of an Ending* (Oxford: Oxford University Press, 1966)

Angela Leighton, *On Form* (Oxford: Oxford University Press, 2007)

Jean-François Lyotard, *The Postmodern Condition* (Manchester: Manchester University Press, 1979)

Vivian Gornick, *The Situation and the Story* (New York: Farrar, Straus and Giroux, 2002)

Linda Hutcheon, *A Poetics of Postmodernism* (London: Routledge, 1988)

Laura Marcus, 'The legacies of modernism', in *The Cambridge Companion to the Modernist Novel* ed. Morag Shiach (Cambridge: Cambridge University Press, 2007)

David Mitchell, *Black Swan Green* (London: Sceptre, 2006)

W. G. Sebald, *The Rings of Saturn* (London: Harvill, 1998)

David Shields, *Reality Hunger: A Manifesto* (London: Hamish Hamilton, 2010)

Ali Smith, *The Accidental* (London: Penguin, 2005)

Oscar Wilde, 'The Critic as Artist', in *Intentions* (Basingstoke: Macmillan, 1919)

Michael Wood, *Literature and the Taste of Knowledge* (Cambridge: Cambridge University Press, 2005)

Virginia Woolf, 'Modern Fiction', in *The Common Reader* (London: Harcourt Brace Jovanovich, 1925)

Chapter 3: Genre

Jorge Luis Borges, 'Kafka and his Precursors', in *Everything and Nothing* (New York: New Directions, 1999)

Toni Morrison, 'Unspeakable things unspoken: The Afro-American presence in American Literature', *Michigan Quarterly Review* (27:1 1989)

Chapter 4: The past

Nicola Barker, *Darkmans* (London: 4th Estate, 2007)

What Historical Novel Do I Read Next? ed. Daniel Burt (Detroit: Gale, 1997)

Javier Cercas, *Soldiers of Salamis* (London: Bloomsbury, 2003)

A. S. Byatt, *On Histories and Stories* (London: Chatto and Windus, 2000)

Jacques Derrida, *Spectres of Marx* trans. Peggy Kamuf (London: Routledge, 1994)

William Golding, *The Hot Gates* (London: Harcourt Brace Jovanovich, 1961)

Maurice Halbwachs, *On Collective Memory* trans. Lewis A. Caser (Chicago: University of Chicago Press, 1992)

Aleksandar Hemon, *The Lazarus Project* (London: Picador, 2008)

György Lukács, *The Historical Novel* trans. Haannah and Styaley Mitchell (London: Penguin, 1962)

Kaye Mitchell, '"That Library of Uncatalogued Pleasure": Queerness, Desire and the Archive in Contemporary Queer Fiction', in *Literatures, Libraries and Archives* ed. Sas Mays (London: Routledge, 2013)

Sarah Waters, *Fingersmith* (London: Virago, 2003)

Hayden White, 'The Burden of History', in *History and Theory*, (5:2) (1966), 111–34

Chapter 5: The present

Aravind Adiga, *The White Tiger* (London: HarperCollins, 2008)

Giorgio Agamben, *Homo Sacer* trans. Daniel Heller-Roazen (Stanford: Stanford University Press, 1998)

Hannah Arendt, *Hannah Arendt/Karl Jaspers Correspondence 1926-1969* (New York: Harcourt Brace Jovanovich, 1992)

Hannah Arendt, *The Origins of Totalitarianism* (New York: Harcourt Brace, 1973)

Jim Crace, *Being Dead* (London: Picador, 2010)

Junot Diaz, *The Brief Wondrous Life of Oscar Wao* (London: Faber and Faber, 2007)

David Eggers and Valentino Achak Deng, *What Is the What: The Autobiography of Valentino Achak Deng* (London: Hamish Hamilton, 2006)

Jonathan Safran Foer, *Extremely Loud and Incredibly Close* (New York: Houghton Mifflin, 2005)

Mohsin Hamid, *The Reluctant Fundamentalist* (London: Penguin, 2007)

Fredric Jameson, 'Third-World Literature in the Era of Multinational Capitalism', in *Social Text* 15 (1986) 65–88

David Keen, *Endless War* (London: Pluto, 2006)

Ian McEwan, *Saturday* (London: Vintage, 2005)

Marilynne Robinson, *Gilead* (London: Virago, 2005)

Salman Rushdie, *Fury* (London: Jonathan Cape, 2001)

Salman Rushdie, *Shalimar the Clown* (London: Jonathan Cape, 2005)

Chapter 6: The future

Jonathan Bate, *The Song of the Earth* (London: Picador, 2000)

Jennifer Egan, *A Visit from the Goon Squad* (London: Corsair, 2010)

Martin Heidegger, 'The Question Concerning Technology', in *Question Concerning Technology and other Essays* (London: HarperPerennial, 1977)

Kazuo Ishiguro, *Never Let Me Go* (London: Faber and Faber, 2005)

David Mitchell, *Cloud Atlas* (London: Sceptre, 2004)

Chapter 7: 'Hey everyone, look at that beautiful thing' / 'Yes, but...'

Geoff Dyer, *Out of Sheer Rage* (London: Picador, 1997)

Further reading

Derek Attridge, *J. M. Coetzee and the Ethics of Reading: Literature in the Event* (Chicago: Chicago University Press and KwaZulu-Natal University Press, 2004)

Derek Attridge, *The Singularity of Literature* (London: Routledge, 2004)

Nick Bentley, *Contemporary British Fiction* (Edinburgh: Edinburgh University Press, 2008)

Arthur Bradley and Andrew Tate, *The New Atheist Novel: Fiction, Philosophy and Polemic after 9/11* (London: Continuum, 2010)

Peter Childs, *Contemporary Novelists: British Fiction since 1970* (London: Palgrave, 2005)

Steven Connor, *The English Novel in History* (London: Routledge, 1996)

Mark Currie, *About Time: Narrative, Fiction and the Philosophy of Time* (Edinburgh: Edinburgh University Press, 2007)

Sarah Dillon, *David Mitchell: Critical Essays* (London: Gylphi, 2011)

Dominic Head, *The State of the Novel* (Oxford: Wiley-Blackwell, 2008)

Dominic Head, *Modern British Fiction, 1950–2000* (Cambridge: Cambridge University Press, 2002)

David James, *Modernist Futures* (Cambridge: Cambridge University Press, 2012)

David James, ed., *The Legacies of Modernism* (Cambridge: Cambridge University Press, 2011)

Frank Kermode, *The Sense of an Ending* (Oxford: Oxford University Press, 1966)

Kay Mitchell, *Intention and Text* (London: Continuum, 2008)

Peter Middleton and Tim Woods, *Literatures of Memory: History, Time and Space in Postwar Writing* (Manchester: Manchester University Press, 2000)

Jago Morrison, *Contemporary Fiction* (London: Routledge, 2003)

Adam Roberts, *The History of Science Fiction* (London: Palgrave, 2006)

Randall Stevenson, Brian McHale, eds, *The Edinburgh Companion to Twentieth-Century Literatures in English* (Edinburgh: Edinburgh University Press, 2006)

Iain Thompson, *Heidegger, Art and Postmodernity* (Cambridge: Cambridge University Press, 2011)

Patricia Waugh, *Blackwell History of British Fiction: 1945–Present* (Oxford: Blackwell, 2009)

Patricia Waugh, *Metafiction: The Theory and Practice of Self-Conscious Fiction* (London: Routledge, 2009)

Julian Young, *Heidegger's Philosophy of Art* (Cambridge: Cambridge University Press, 2001)

Journals

C21 Literature: Journal of 21st-Century Writings: http://www.gylphi.co.uk/c21/index.php

Alluvium: http://www.alluvium-journal.org/

Index

Expand your collection of
VERY SHORT INTRODUCTIONS

SOCIAL MEDIA
Very Short Introduction

Join our community
www.oup.com/vsi

- Join us online at the official Very Short Introductions **Facebook** page.
- Access the thoughts and musings of our authors with our online **blog**.
- Sign up for our monthly **e-newsletter** to receive information on all new titles publishing that month.
- Browse the full range of Very Short Introductions online.
- Read **extracts** from the Introductions for free.
- Visit our library of **Reading Guides**. These guides, written by our expert authors will help you to question again, why you think what you think.
- If you are a teacher or lecturer you can order inspection copies quickly and simply via our website.

ONLINE CATALOGUE
A Very Short Introduction

Our online catalogue is designed to make it easy to find your ideal Very Short Introduction. View the entire collection by subject area, watch author videos, read sample chapters, and download reading guides.